ALLEN COUNTY PUBLIC LIBRARY

P9-AFS-410

"Stay."

Simon didn't let go of her arm, though his business associates were waiting for him. They'd already staked out a table in the bar, and were looking at Simon questioningly.

"I—I don't know..." Sarah mumbled.

"Please." His voice was low, with a husky catch at the end. Or maybe that was desperation. All Simon knew was that he needed to be with her just now. He couldn't remember the last time he'd felt that way.

She was so...something. Simon found himself terribly attracted to her in this incarnation. She was hot. Totally hot. Look-at-me hot. And Simon looked. He couldn't stop looking.

What he *needed* to do was pay attention to his potential clients. Negotiations had reached a delicate stage at which the slightest thing could make them go either way. Simon had already lost two accounts this week. Losing this one after all the time they'd invested would be no good for the bottom line.

Still, his eyes glued on Sarah, all he could think about was that directly above them were floors filled with many, many beds.

And he needed only one.

JAN 2 1 2004

ROMANCE

Dear Reader,

A few months ago I was at a bridal shower, where the topic naturally turned to men. And surprisingly, I discovered there were two categories of women at the shower—well, other than the bride-to-be, who was in a category all by herself, and myself (who is happily married, thank you very much). But as for the others, all the women fell into two groups—the career singles (those who are single and loving it) and the singles who'd made a career out of preparing for marriage.

As the bride opened her presents, there was a friendly yet intense discussion about life and men—specifically whether or not these women actually wanted a man in their lives...and then how to get him there if they did. When they talked strategies, the career singles and the seriously-getting-marrieds sounded a lot like my characters Hayden and Missy. And I couldn't help thinking that the perfect girlfriend would be someone who was a mix of the two....

That's how my heroine Sara came to be. I hope you enjoy her adventures in *How To Be the Perfect Girlfriend*. Who knows? Maybe you'll pick up some tips!

Don't forget to stop by www.HeatherMacAllister.com for news about upcoming books.

Happy reading!

Heather MacAllister

Books by Heather MacAllister

HARLEQUIN TEMPTATION

HEATHER MacALLISTER

HOW TO BE THE PERFECT GIRLFRIEND

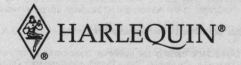

HARLEQUIN®

TORONTO • NEW YORK • LONDON
AMSTERDAM • PARIS • SYDNEY • HAMBURG
STOCKHOLM • ATHENS • TOKYO • MILAN • MADRID
PRAGUE • WARSAW • BUDAPEST • AUCKLAND

If you purchased this book without a cover you should be aware that this book is stolen property. It was reported as "unsold and destroyed" to the publisher, and neither the author nor the publisher has received any payment for this "stripped book."

My thanks to perfect girlfriends
Candace Cogan and Hellen Knox, who acted as
my husband's personal chauffeurs and let him
boss them around so I could stay home and write this book.

ISBN 0-373-69159-9

HOW TO BE THE PERFECT GIRLFRIEND

Copyright © 2004 by Heather W. MacAllister.

All rights reserved. Except for use in any review, the reproduction or utilization of this work in whole or in part in any form by any electronic, mechanical or other means, now known or hereafter invented, including xerography, photocopying and recording, or in any information storage or retrieval system, is forbidden without the written permission of the publisher, Harlequin Enterprises Limited, 225 Duncan Mill Road, Don Mills, Ontario, Canada M3B 3K9.

All characters in this book have no existence outside the imagination of the author and have no relation whatsoever to anyone bearing the same name or names. They are not even distantly inspired by any individual known or unknown to the author, and all incidents are pure invention.

This edition published by arrangement with Harlequin Books S.A.

® and TM are trademarks of the publisher. Trademarks indicated with ® are registered in the United States Patent and Trademark Office, the Canadian Trade Marks Office and in other countries.

Visit us at www.eHarlequin.com

Printed in U.S.A.

1

THERE WAS NOTHING like a little humiliation to get the blood flowing on an ordinary Tuesday morning. Sara Lipton's came in the form of rejection by e-mail. It was a new personal low.

Somehow, e-mail rejection was more humiliating than rejection by answering machine, and oh, yes, she'd had plenty of experience with that kind.

In this case, she'd sent a carefully casual, yet sensually perky—and don't think that was easy to achieve—e-mail to the visiting business associate with whom she'd spent several enjoyable hours last Friday night.

And this was his response: *I can't seem to locate you in my client base—have we met?* And then to hammer home the point, he'd signed it, *Bradley Whit, Senior Software Consultant, Cynoware Industries.*

Oh, they'd met. Their lips had met, too. Several times in a dark corner booth long after the rest of the gang from work had left. In fact, Sara thought Bradley had been kissing her in a we've-clicked-and-I-want-to-see-you-again way, when it apparently was an I'm-in-town-from-Boston-and-am-looking-for-temporary-fun-in-Houston way.

Yeah, and she'd given him a real Texas welcome. Or would that be a French welcome? Better not go there.

Have we met? This was fast becoming the story of her life. Okay, then. It was time to rewrite the story of her life.

And she intended to, just as soon as she finished photocopying the end-of-month employee evaluations. Clutching them to her as though they contained Avalli Digital Media's most sacred company secrets— she was a little worried about the new privacy policy— Sara left her cubicle and headed down the hall.

She'd hoped to finish copying them by lunchtime because she'd called her friend and co-worker Hayden to meet her for a heart-to-heart chat about Life and Men. Mostly men—Hayden's area of expertise. Sara didn't want to be late because she'd also asked Missy, the cute little blond temp from Dallas who got on Hayden's nerves because all she ever discussed was her upcoming wedding. Yeah, so sue her. Sara was fascinated by the details. Go figure.

Between them Sara figured these two women knew everything worth knowing about men. Hayden could give her tips on how to get a man, and Missy could tell her what to do with him once she got him. A perfect plan, if Sara did say so herself.

There was a line at the photocopier and Sara couldn't wait until after lunch, which meant she was going to be late. Whipping out her cell phone, she called Hayden, hoping to catch her before she left for the café.

"Where are you?" was the way Hayden answered the phone. From the background noise, Sara could tell that she was already in the building's atrium café.

"Can you grab us a table? I'm caught at the photocopier."

"Can't you just scan and print?"

"No. You know we don't want confidential information on the network."

"I swear. You people in payroll are paranoid. Hey— you just need black-and-whites, right?"

"Yeah."

"Then go on up to my floor. There's an old machine that we keep next to the vending machines. It doesn't collate or do anything fancy, but you'll get your copies."

"I'm on my way." Sara pulled open the door to the stairs and started running up the two flights to the twenty-sixth floor, her steps echoing in the stairwell.

The running lasted half a flight. She really needed to start exercising.

Breathing heavily, Sara found the old machine in the deserted vending area of the marketing department. All the marketing people apparently ate lunch out. If Sara had an expense account, she'd eat out all the time, too. But payroll assistants didn't have expense accounts. Sara brown-bagged her lunch at least two days a week and aimed for three. It was part of her long-range plan to become fiscally responsible. See? She was planning for the future. She was maturing.

She deserved a mature relationship. One with commitment at its core. A life-partner relationship.

Either that or a lot of really fun, hot, immature relationships. Relationshipettes, maybe. Memorable encounters, even. The kind that inspired women to write memoirs. Sara visualized herself with silver hair, gnarled hands weighed down with diamonds and a satisfied smile as she dictated her life story to a fascinated and envious young woman.

Right. At this point, both visions seemed extremely far-fetched. She was neither fabulously single nor contentedly married. She wasn't even contentedly single and fabulously married. No, Sara was discontentedly unmarried.

There was a difference between being single and being unmarried. Single had a proactive sound and implied a life of fun dates and attractive men at one's beck and call. There had never been a man at Sara's beck and no one had called in far too long.

Lately, Sara had found the idea of being part of a committed couple increasingly appealing. She'd done the casual relationship thing—that is, all her relationships had been casual as far as the men were concerned—and now she wanted to experience the novelty of having a male completely devoted to her. Solely to her.

A love slave would be nice, or at least a man who put her first instead of bowling night with his friends, and who actually checked with her before accepting an invitation to the Astros game, which he went to without her instead of taking her to the art film he'd kinda sorta promised he would that night and then not even realizing why she was mad....

Well, anyway, Sara wanted someone different from her usual sort of man. Maybe it was because she was staring thirty in the face, or maybe it was something as shallow as buying all those wedding shower gifts at Williams Sonoma when she couldn't afford to buy anything for herself there, but Sara had experienced definite coupling urges. Unfortunately, there was no one to couple with.

The old machine was humming along nicely and Sara was manually collating as she went when there was an ominous whirring and everything stopped. The paper-jam light blinked. It figured. Unfortunately, Sara couldn't see any scrunched-up paper. In frustration, she put down her papers and called Hayden.

"Does the stupid machine ever jam on you?"

"It jammed for real? Oh, you lucky girl."

"What?"

Hayden's voice turned husky. "You get to call Simon."

"I don't have time to wait for a repair guy."

"No—Simon Northrup."

"You mean *Mr. Northrup?*" Only Hayden could get away with bothering a company vice president with something like this. But then men treated Hayden differently than they treated the rest of the female population.

"Oh, yes." Hayden sighed. "I've been known to use

a rubber band and a staple to jam the copier just so I can watch him lean over the machine."

"Hayden, you are a sick woman."

"He wears European-cut slacks and he wears them very well."

Hayden's voice was so loud that Sara looked over her shoulder in case there was someone to overhear. "I can't bother Mr. Northrup. Besides, he's probably already gone to lunch."

"He never goes to lunch this early."

"I'll just figure out how to unjam the thing myself. Oh, uh, I asked Missy to join us, so don't wander off. Bye!" Sara hurriedly disconnected before Hayden could protest.

She opened the side door of the big old machine and peered at the copier's guts. Yeah, there was the paper scrunched way back in there. Stretching her arm through and getting a black toner smear on her blouse, Sara found she couldn't reach the paper. Great. She was either going to have to go in from the top, and it didn't look as though she could reach the jam that way either, or pull the thing out from the wall. It was wedged between the Coke machine and the coffee bar.

Or she was going to have to—

"Ah. Another jam." A tall man wearing cool techno glasses strode across the break room. "Sometimes I wonder why we keep this machine." It was Simon Northrup.

Sara had seen him before, of course, but had never actually spoken to him. He'd always seemed a little remote and kind of intimidating, but the smile he gave her was friendly enough.

"Yeah, it, uh, jammed." Brilliant, brilliant.

"Let's take a look." He set his coffee mug on the counter next to Sara and unbuttoned the cuffs of his blinding white shirt.

Custom, Sara thought, without ever having knowingly seen a custom-tailored shirt. Nice. More men should go custom. Maybe *she* should go custom.

"It's a great old warhorse," he nodded to the machine, "so I suppose we can allow it this one eccentricity."

Eccentricity. Each letter sounded crisply. Sara could listen to him talk all day. Since she dealt with personnel records, she knew Simon Northrup was from Boston and had gone to boarding school in England. The resulting accent might not be as noticeable up North, but in Texas the clipped edges and slightly formal word choice contrasted with the good-ole-boy twang she heard all the time. Contrasted in a good way. A sexy way. She was beginning to see why he appealed to Hayden.

As he rolled up his sleeves, Simon asked, "Are you a new employee? A temp?"

Gritting her teeth, Sara sighed inwardly. Unmemorable. That's what she was.

"Wait—I've seen you before, haven't I?" He studied her, his head tilted slightly in a way that emphasized his square jaw.

If Hayden hadn't gone on about him, Sara would

never have noticed the square jaw. "I'm Sara Lipton from payroll. I was trying to avoid the wait at our machine."

"Well, we'll see if we can't get you back in business here."

Sleeves rolled up to reveal arms more tanned than she'd expected, Simon closed the side door Sara had opened, raised the heavy top section and leaned over the machine.

From then on, Sara saw everything in slow motion...the way his shirt clung to him as he bent over the machine and reached inside; the way his flanks stretched; his hips flexed and the fabric of his dark slacks stretched, smoothed, outlined and emphasized his fabulous behind....

Oh, boy, did it emphasize. Sara inhaled deeply. Simon's rear end was indeed a thing of beauty. She was an immediate European-cut convert. Who knew?

She swallowed, aware of a nearly irresistible urge to touch it. No, not touch...grab. Manhandle, as it were. It was a revelation. Was this the way men felt about women?

"The paper isn't jammed in the normal spot," Simon said from inside the copier.

Sara thought of Hayden's deliberate jamming which she now not only understood, but applauded. "I really appreciate you taking the time to fix it." *Take all the time you want.*

Simon raised himself slightly to glance at her over his shoulder. Sara nearly whimpered when the movement shifted his hips, resulting in the perfect calendar shot. Man and machine.

Actually, just the man was plenty.

"My pleasure," he said before turning back.

The pleasure is all mine. Sara had picked up her employee evaluations and gripped them closely to her chest. She hadn't thought she was the type to appreciate a man's physical attributes à la carte like this. Usually, she accepted or rejected the whole package, not that Simon's total package was anything to reject. It was just that there were some spectacular, uh, aspects to consider. So she considered them carefully, even while acknowledging that this package was not for her. Undoubtedly, some other woman unwrapped it at night.

"Got it." He straightened and tossed two scraps of paper into the wastebasket.

"Thanks." Sara would retrieve them later. Her department now shredded all document-related trash to ensure privacy.

Simon washed his hands at the sink, then poured a mug of coffee. "Happy copying," he said on his way out before she could say anything memorably brilliant.

Omigosh, omigosh, omigosh. How could this man have been working just two floors away from her for the past year?

Okay. Calm down. Realistically Simon Northrup was not her type. Or rather, she wasn't his type. She didn't have the...the *something* men who looked like that required in their women.

Hayden had it. In fact Hayden had too much of it.

Missy had a younger version of it.

And Sara was going to do her best to get it.

She retrieved the paper and hurriedly finished her copying. She was going to have to use this machine more often.

When Sara made it downstairs to the lobby of the Perkins building, she saw Hayden and Missy sitting at one of the glass-topped tables in the atrium near the fountain. They already had salads and there was a third one for her. Missy was showing Hayden a magazine. From Hayden's bored expression, Sara knew it was a bridal magazine. At least they hadn't strangled each other yet.

"I don't see what the problem is," Hayden was saying as Sara got within earshot.

"The blue is the problem!" Missy reached into the tote bag she carried everywhere—the official Melissa and Peter Wedding Tote. It had once been a pristine white, but was now looking a little shopworn. Missy had been engaged for a year and a half while she planned the ultimate wedding.

She held up a wad of fabric swatches. "I have to make a decision soon and not one of these matches the Jordan almonds!"

"So have them custom dyed. I know a company that will dye them any color you want. They can even match your baby blue eyes."

"Don't encourage her," Sara murmured under her breath as she slid into a chair.

Hayden had a dangerous sparkle in her eye. "In fact, they'll even inscribe Melissa and Peter or the date on each individual almond."

Missy's eyes widened. "They will?"

"In gold or silver if you want."

"Oh..." Missy stared off into the distance, her expression approaching rapture, as she added personalized almonds to her wedding vision.

They'd seen her zone out before and undoubtedly would again. Sara leveled a look at the unrepentant Hayden.

Moments later, Missy returned from wedding Valhalla. "Okay." She clicked her pen. "What's the name of the company?"

"Bridal Sweets," Hayden told her. "I'll have to look them up and get back to you."

"Hayden, you're a doll. Thanks!" Missy beamed at her. Hayden smiled back.

Sara was sure the world would stop spinning. "Okay, now that Missy's almond problem is taken care of, I'd like you both to turn your attention to me."

"That won't be any fun," Hayden muttered.

"Mr. Northrup fixed my paper jam," Sara said to taunt her.

"Mmm." Hayden closed her eyes. "And did you enjoy it?"

"Oh, yes. It took a while because the jam was way in the back."

They both exhaled.

"What are you two talking about?" Missy asked.

"Never mind, you're engaged," Sara said. "Which is why you're here. You're on the Super Corporate Wife track and from watching you these past few months, I can see that it isn't something that just happens." Sara figured a little buttering up couldn't hurt. "You've got to go after it, and the man who can make that kind of life happen. It takes work. And you have worked. Most efficiently."

Missy dimpled, something Sara would never be able to do. "Why thank you, Sara. I think that's the nicest thing you've ever said to me. I'm glad somebody appreciates everything I've done to achieve what I have," she added with a glance at Hayden.

"Whatever floats your boat, honey," Hayden said and crossed her legs as a TDH—tall, dark and handsome—walked past.

The movement caught the man's attention and he checked out Hayden's legs, then met her eyes, all while carrying on a conversation with the man next to him.

"And that would be why you're here, Hayden."

"You need my sophisticated style and wit?"

"I want to know how you can attract anything with a Y-chromosome."

Hayden gave a smile that visually purred. "With the sophisticated style and wit I just mentioned."

After a glance at Hayden's climbing hemline, Missy raised her eyebrows. "We call that something else where I come from."

"No doubt because you lack sophisticated style and wit," Hayden drawled.

"Hey!" Sara signaled a time-out. "Can we please focus on me? I need help with the man/woman thing. I'm not doing it right."

"I didn't think you were doing it at all."

Sara gritted her teeth. "Well, that would be the problem, Hayden." She inhaled, knowing she was going to have to tell them everything. "I'm not hooking up with the right kind of men and when I do, I'm Teflon woman—they don't stick around." She told them about Mr. Kiss-and-Run from Friday night.

"Well, it's no wonder—you were making out with him in a public place!" Missy lowered her voice. "A *bar*. He thought you were one of *those* kind of women and didn't take you seriously."

"I've found that men take that sort of thing *very* seriously," Hayden said.

"So why did he pretend not to know her? My mama always said, men won't buy the cow if they can get the milk for free."

Hayden rolled her eyes. "They'll just get the milk from another cow."

"I didn't give him any milk," Sara pointed out.

"Maybe that was the problem."

Missy glared at Hayden. "Well, maybe if all the cows got together and agreed to stop giving milk—"

"They'd end up as hamburger."

"Not if they chose their herd carefully," Missy snapped.

"Who cares about the herd? Pay attention to the bull."

"That is just so typical of you."

Hayden blinked. "Moo."

"This is not helping," Sara said.

"What did you expect?" Missy speared a tomato wedge in her salad so hard she broke a tine on her plastic fork.

"I was hoping for help in attracting men from Hayden and figuring out which *ones* to attract and how to keep them from you."

Missy got all huffy. "*I* can attract men! But I'm engaged, so I choose not to."

"Right," Hayden said.

"I can!" Missy glanced around, then peeled off her sweater revealing a tight black sleeveless shell. Then she turned her diamond engagement ring around to hide the stone.

Sara had no idea how big the diamond was, only that when the light caught the stone and it flashed, the reflection left a blue-green dot in her vision.

After fluffing her blond hair and throwing back her shoulders, Missy waited a couple of beats, then picked up the broken fork and gasped. "Oh, no! My fork broke!"

Oh, please. Sara rolled her eyes so hard she felt the muscles twinge.

And yet, there was an instant response. "Here, take mine," said a man from the next table at the same moment another passing by handed her one from his tray.

"Here you go." Then he just stood there.

Smiling widely, Missy took the fork. "Why, aren't

you both so sweet," she gushed as only a Texas belle could.

"I need a fork, too," Sara said. No one even blinked. But then, she hadn't expected them to.

Missy held the attention of the men with her smile long enough to make her point, then released them by turning back to her salad. The man with the tray looked as if he wanted to linger, so Missy tucked her hair behind her ear, the flashing diamond visible once more.

Very neatly done. Disappointment crossed the man's face and he left. Missy shrugged back into her sweater.

"Not bad," admitted Hayden. "Just don't try going one on one with me."

"I doubt that'll happen." Missy's voice was lethally sweet. "We don't move in the same social circles."

"I'm not moving in *any* social circles!" Sara dropped her head to the table. "I give up."

"But you haven't started yet," Missy said.

"What's the point? I'll never be able to stop men in their tracks the way you and Hayden do."

"But do you truly want to?" Hayden asked.

Sara raised her head just high enough to prop it on her fist. "Maybe not stop so much as slow them down."

"And then what?" Missy asked.

"What do you mean 'and then what'?"

"What are you going to do with them when you've got them?"

"Well, I don't know. I was hoping we could talk about that after I found somebody."

"I think that's been your problem. We should be talking about afterward before."

"Huh?"

Missy reached into her wedding tote, withdrew a Palm Pilot and unfolded a keyboard for it. "You need a goal and a plan to reach it." She looked at Hayden. "Am I right?"

"Yes." Hayden crossed her arms over her chest and watched the parade of men coming down the escalator. "Much as I hate to admit it."

Missy's fingers were poised over the keyboard. "So, what do you want, Sara?"

Well, this was it and she'd better pay attention. "I want a man who's interested in making a life with me."

Missy started typing. "Marriage."

Hayden snorted.

"Or at least long-term devotion. Long-term enough for me to decide if I want it to lead to marriage," Sara added because she didn't want to completely alienate Hayden with marriage talk. "Certainly a better caliber of man."

"What kind of man do you want?" Hayden asked, as though it were that simple.

"The perfect man, of course," Sara said flippantly.

"Then you'll have to become the perfect woman." Missy was serious.

"Oh, sure. Why didn't I think of that? I'll get right on it." Sara slapped her hands on the table and looked around the atrium. "Anybody seen my fairy god-mother?"

"Snippy, snippy." Melissa typed something.

"Calm down, Sara." Hayden stopped casing the escalator for men and closed her plastic salad container. "Perfection is the way you define it. Missy has her idea of the perfect man, I have mine and you should have yours."

"And then you have to become his match." Missy eyed her, then typed some more.

Sara eyed Missy right back. "Now, wait a minute—I am *not* becoming one of those women who completely changes herself for a man."

"All we're saying is if you want a pilot, you hang out around airplanes. You don't want a bowler, then stay out of bowling alleys." Hayden leaned sideways trying to see what Missy was typing.

"Oh." That made sense.

"Good Lord, she's started a spreadsheet." Hayden grinned at Sara. "You should see what's in the 'improvements' column."

"Sara said she wanted to upgrade her men."

"I just thought you'd teach me a secret handshake and tell me to wear a padded bra," Sara grumbled. Why had she thought this would be as simple as a few tips over lunch?

"Excuse me!" Missy gestured to her chest. "There is nothing padded here. That's...that's false advertising."

"There is nothing false about my advertising, honey," Hayden snapped.

"Hello?" Sara waved her hands. "Me? Focus on me!"

Hayden grabbed her hands. "Nails."

"Oh, I know," Missy tut-tutted. "Acrylic?"

"Hmm." Both Hayden and Missy looked at Sara.

She pulled her hands away and resisted the urge to sit on them.

Hayden laughed. "Let's just go for groomed right now."

"Oh, thanks a lot."

"What about her hair?" Missy tossed her mane of one hundred and fifty dollar highlights over her shoulder. "Except I really shouldn't fill that in if she wants a low-maintenance man."

Sara wasn't sure, but she thought there was an insult in there.

"Sara, you're going to have to give us specifics on the kind of man you want." Missy waited expectantly.

"Well...he should be kind, honest and have a sense of humor—"

"Yeah, yeah, we all want those." Hayden made a hurry-up gesture. "Add sexy." She smiled at Sara. "My little gift to you."

"I'm going to type all those in," Missy said. "Later, you'll have to rank the traits."

"What is this?" Even though she'd asked for help, she hadn't expected them to be quite this helpful. "Are you running a dating service?"

Missy ignored her. "Possible professions?"

"I don't know—professional."

Missy typed. "More."

"Probably older than me. Mature. Never married—or at least no children. I don't want to do the stepmother thing."

"Completely understandable," Hayden agreed. "Go on."

"I—" Sara thought of Bradley from Friday night. Why had she thought he was attractive? "Classy. Someone who enjoys dining occasionally, rather than just hitting all the fast food places in town. A man who might like to cook, even, or at least take a class with me. Someone who knows how to use all the silverware and doesn't make jokes about the spork being the perfect utensil."

"Now we're getting somewhere," Hayden said. "What else?"

"Cultured. Refined. Elegant." Now she was thinking of Ryan, her last boyfriend, who had been none of those things. She was describing the anti-Ryan. Well? Wasn't that the idea? "A man who'd appreciate seeing a play, or going to the symphony, or...an art gallery. And money. I don't want to have to lend him money. And his car should be nice. It doesn't have to be expensive, it just has to work. And he should be the type of man who'd walk me to the door and pull out my chair and buy my mother a corsage for Mother's Day because he's just so damn happy she had me."

Missy had stopped typing. Sara was aware that she and Hayden were staring at her. "What?"

"Anything else?" Hayden asked.

"He should dress well. You know, somebody who actually owns a suit and doesn't need help tying his tie and isn't color-blind. Oh, and he shouldn't freak out when he sees a wine list in a restaurant."

"Is that all?" Hayden wore a funny smile.

"Yes—no. He should know how to dance."

"The Cotton-Eyed Joe?"

"No, real dancing."

Missy gasped. "Bite your tongue!"

"Okay, he would be willing to dance the Cotton-Eyed Joe if we were ever in a place where people were dancing it. But I was just thinking that it would be nice if he knew how to dance the kind of dances that get played at weddings when the bride and groom get the first dance and then the bridesmaids have to dance and it's really awful if your partner can't dance because everyone is staring at you and you trip over the stupid dress."

"I ran out of room," Missy said. "I should have brought my laptop."

Hayden studied Sara. "And is that everything about your ideal man?"

Sara thought. "He should be well-spoken and use correct grammar." Hey, it would make her mother happy.

"Maybe even with a slight accent?" Hayden asked.

"Accents can be cool."

Hayden laughed. "I guess so because, Sara, sweetie, you have just described Simon Northrup."

2

SIMON NORTHRUP was having a bad day. He knew it when the highlight had been fixing a paper jam. The afternoon had gone downhill from there. Not one, but two, count 'em two, accounts had gone to rival companies. Yes, the paper jam had definitely been the best part. And the girl—woman, female or whatever the politically correct term was these days—was the sole reason the paper jam was a highlight.

Until he remembered that he wasn't supposed to be having female highlights. He had enough trouble with the females in his life as it was. He needed to keep his eyes in front and his mind blank.

But he couldn't. She'd had brown eyes. Soft brown hair. A quiet, conservative manner. Such a refreshing change from most Texas women who were all woman and let a man know it at every opportunity and expected said man to acknowledge their womanliness constantly. In-your-face-female pulchritude. For some men, sexual nirvana. For Simon, who had temporarily forsworn women, torture. Texas women were so much *effort*. As he had cause to know, they were well worth that effort. But restful they definitely were not.

The photocopier woman looked restful. Truthfully,

in his more active dating days, he might have over-looked her. How ironic that now that he'd noticed her, it would do him no good to dwell on the eyes and the hair and the soft voice and the slim, discreetly covered body and the thought of finally finding a female who could just be and not feel compelled to fill the silence with chattering or discussing or arguing or comment-ing or complaining or fussing.

Simon hated it when women fussed over him. Some men really got off on that, but he liked to solve his own problems. If he wanted advice, he'd ask for it.

Simon took off his glasses and rubbed the places on either side of his nose where the pads fit. His new glasses were trendy, but uncomfortable. Wasn't that al-ways the way?

Sara from payroll hadn't been wearing glasses, but if she had been, he imagined she'd go for comfort over style.

But he shouldn't be thinking about her. Kayla gave him plenty to think about.

Simon exhaled. Were relationships supposed to be this much work?

As penance, he impulsively picked up the phone and dialed her number.

"Hey, Simon," she answered. "What's up?"

He hated caller ID. "I'm just checking in. Do you want to have dinner with me tonight?"

There was silence. Or rather, Kayla didn't speak. Simon could hear loud music in the background, the kind Kayla liked to play in his car. The kind he didn't like.

"Will you have any businesspeople with you?"

Kayla didn't do well in the corporate entertaining arena. He was unlikely to make the mistake of bringing her along on business dinners again. "No, it's just you and me, kiddo. But you still get to dress up."

"Yeah, okay I guess," she said at last. The way she said it told Simon she was in a mood. Lately, Kayla was always in a mood. At first, Simon had wasted a lot of mental energy trying to discover the source of these moods, but he had since learned that it was best to ride them out.

Or order two desserts. What was it about women not ever ordering their own desserts? Where was it written that dessert had to be shared? Simon had realized the key was to order a dessert, pretend not to like it and give it to Kayla. Then order another one and give up half of that, too.

It made Kayla happy and mellow and they had very good times together when Kayla was happy and mellow.

They made arrangements for her to meet him at his office. In the meantime, he could return phone calls and do some scut work so he wouldn't have to come in so early tomorrow.

He grabbed a stack of expense account receipts and headed for the copy machine wondering on the way how Sara felt about desserts.

"SIMON NORTHRUP?" Sara shook her head. "No way."

"Why not?"

"Well, he's, well...he's old." She didn't know how old, but she could find out if it became necessary.

"Not that old," Hayden said chillingly.

Oops. Sometimes Sara forgot that Hayden was over thirty. She could find out how far over, if she wanted, but she wouldn't. Hayden was a friend. Snooping wouldn't be right.

Not to mention against company policy.

"I don't know." Missy stared at the tiny screen.

"Well, I do." Hayden was in a huff.

Puzzled by the tone in her voice, Missy looked up, then batted her hand. "I meant that Sara said she didn't want a man who had children and there have been rumors that Simon Northrup has been spending a lot of time with a woman who has a daughter."

"An ex?" Sara shouldn't have said anything.

Sure enough, Hayden's eyebrow arched. "You should be so lucky. Simon doesn't have an ex. Therefore, this is a current and fairly well-entrenched relationship, if he's met her child. Too bad."

"I wasn't considering him anyway." She knew nobody believed her. But she wasn't, she told herself. Nope. But even *she* didn't believe herself.

"Well, it makes sense that he's already in a relationship," Hayden said. "Since he was totally unresponsive."

"To whom?" Missy asked with precision.

Hayden gave her a look.

"*You* went for him?" Sara grappled with the image of a Simon/Hayden pairing.

"Well, I—"

"And he rejected *you*?" Well, that was it. If Simon had rejected Hayden, Sara didn't stand a chance. Not that she wanted a chance. Not really.

"Reject is such a harsh word. We didn't click, that's all."

"Still, she can practice on him," Missy said. "Talk to him and see what his interests are. Flirt a little."

"What's the point of that?" Sara asked.

"To see what his reaction is," Hayden answered. "Then you'll know how to approach men of his type. And, honey, you did describe his type."

Had she? Had she described a man so out of her league as her ideal man? This was not looking good. "Do you really think I should practice on him?"

Hayden and Missy both nodded. At least they didn't laugh.

"How am I supposed to approach him, anyway? He's a vice president. It's not like I'm going to run across him at Happy Hour or that he'll have a sudden urge to get coffee from the twenty-fourth floor."

"No, but there's always the photocopier. You've set a precedent."

"Won't he catch on?"

"I hope not." Hayden fanned herself.

"I am going to have to go to the twenty-sixth floor and copy something," Missy said.

"You're engaged," Sara reminded her, not happy with the idea of Missy in Simon's line of vision.

"So it's settled," Hayden said.

Sara didn't feel settled at all. "If he's uninterested, then how am I supposed to judge his reaction?"

"You'll know," Missy said. "He may not choose to act, but you'll still know."

Hayden smiled. "Just watch for the gleam in his eye."

Okay, sure. She'd just watch for the old gleam in his eye. Had she ever seen a gleam in a man's eye? Sara wondered when she was back at her desk. Men must look at Hayden differently than they looked at her. Even Missy had known about the gleam. Sara must be in worse shape than she thought.

She was sitting at her desk stuffing pay envelopes when there was a discreet knock on her cubicle wall. To her complete astonishment, she looked up and saw Simon Northrup.

That rotten Hayden must have said something to him. How mortifying.

"Hello." Once more Simon's accent—what little of it that could be squeezed into one word—washed over her.

That wasn't the only thing washing over her. A gigantic blush began in her chest and bloomed upward.

He'd gotten better-looking in the last few hours. "Sara, isn't it?"

Holy cow. Sara, tongue paralyzed, nodded. *Do not*

think about cows. Flirt with Simon Northrup. Engage him in conversation. Oh, she was doing *so* well.

"I found this in the photocopier." He held up a piece of paper.

And just as quickly as she'd blushed, she felt the heat drain away.

The paper Simon held was an original of one of the employee evaluations she'd been copying before lunch. The ultimate confidential material. And she'd apparently left it lying in the copier for anyone to see.

Such a mistake could cost her her job. Instant dismissal. No second chances. Simon had to have known and yet, rather than returning the paper to personnel and prompting an inquiry, he'd brought it to her.

She took the paper noting that the edges trembled. "This shouldn't have happened. I feel terrible."

He gazed down at her, his brown eyes—sans glasses—slightly warmer than polite, but definitely without a gleam. Not that she should be looking for a gleam right now. Or even thinking gleaming thoughts.

"No harm done. I discovered it sitting there on the glass, so I don't think anyone else used the machine after you did."

Sara exhaled, sagging with relief. Still dealing with the enormity of her confidentiality breach, she could only nod.

She never made mistakes like this. Never. She'd been in a hurry and she'd been thinking about Simon, or certain parts of him, and look what had happened.

Now she should say something, but it didn't seem like the time to flirt.

Still, couldn't she come up with something witty? She stared at the paper in her hands as though there would be something witty to share about Charles Lufkin, who, according to his evaluation, arrived at work promptly and left just as promptly and who performed with satisfactory adequacy.

A real firecracker, that Charles. Nothing like a reality check of the males currently out there to make her appreciate the one standing in front of her. She scoured her uncooperative—and certainly inadequate—brain for something to say. At this point, she'd abandoned any thoughts of wittiness.

She drew a breath and prepared to meet Simon's eyes.

He was gone.

Oh, great. Fabulous. She almost started after him to thank him, but knew she'd better wait until she calmed down and thought up something to say to him.

Sara put Charles Lufkin's evaluation on the stack she had yet to file. Imagine that: Simon Northrup, the legendary by-the-book Simon Northrup, had saved her job. He'd taken the time to hand deliver the paper. He hadn't called her supervisor in the payroll department to come and get it. He hadn't called *her* to come and get it.

He'd brought it to her, himself.

How incredibly kind.

Sara heard a faint mental "ding" and realized that

kindness was a trait she'd ascribed to her ideal man. And he'd been kind to her twice today.

If she weren't careful, she'd find herself with a big, fat crush on Simon. Today had certainly put him in a different, and much more attractive, light. How could she ever have thought him intimidating and stuck-up? Stuck-up people didn't fix paper jams—real or manufactured—for others and they sure didn't cover for an underling's mistake the way he had.

By the end of the day, Sara was not surprised to recognize crush symptoms, which meant that flirting with Simon for practice was now out of the question. Practice flirting only worked when emotions weren't involved. So, no flirting. At least for practice—no, no, *no*. No flirting *at all*. She'd have to find another man of that type for practice. With Simon, it was professional contact only. And maybe a lot of paper jams.

Since she hadn't properly thanked him, Sara screwed up her courage and climbed up to the twenty-sixth floor to stop by his office and basically say, "I owe you." Like he'd ever collect. Still, it was the professional thing to do.

The twenty-sixth floor was definitely more plush than hers, Sara thought when she stepped off the elevator. The carpet was thicker, the colors more modern and the furniture trendier. Client photographs and media stills lined the elevator bays. The receptionist appeared to have already left for the day. Sara knew where Hayden's office was, but she wasn't sure about Simon's. He probably had an office with windows, which meant if she stuck to the outer perimeter, sooner or later she'd eventually stumble across it.

It was sooner rather than later and there was no stumbling involved.

She heard him talking on the phone and stopped to listen for a moment and gather her thoughts. There weren't a lot of thoughts to gather, considering she'd had all day to think about what to say to him. "Thank you" was heartfelt and sincere, but once it was said and he responded politely, there wouldn't be a whole lot left to say.

She heard him return the phone to its cradle and stepped into the doorway. "Mr. Northrup?"

He was standing behind his desk and there was a flash in his eyes. A flash, not a gleam, and it only meant he recognized her. "Sara."

"I, uh..." *Don't say "uh."* "I—"

The phone buzzed. He frowned, let two buzzes go by then held up a finger indicating that Sara should stay.

She hated that, hated waiting around while someone was on the phone, pretending that she couldn't hear, when of course she could. Even worse was when the conversation took an unexpected turn and she had to decide if she'd continue to pretend to be oblivious, or leave.

She really didn't have much to say to Simon. She could just mouth her thank-you and make her escape except...

Except Simon had reached for the phone without

breaking eye contact. How sexy was that? He didn't mean for it to be sexy, she told herself. He couldn't help it.

She swallowed.

Simon continued gazing at her as he spoke into the phone. If she had to describe his expression, she'd say it was watchful. The weird thing was that she didn't feel at all uncomfortable or awkward about it.

So she gazed—it wasn't really staring—back at him. Only at his eyes. Warm chocolate velvet eyes. Awareness crept over her. Awareness of him. Awareness of her. Awareness of what could be.

Awareness that she was probably making way too big a deal of this. But then people with big, fat crushes on other people did that, didn't they?

"Yes," he said. "Ask them to come up." A pause, then, "How many?" He blinked for the first time. Just once. "I see. Yes, it's all right." He hung up the phone as smoothly as he'd answered it. "Sorry about that."

"Oh, no. I know you're busy. I just wanted to say thanks for not making a big deal out of finding the paper." She thought about the way that sounded. "Not that it *isn't* a big deal, and I know it. And I want you to know that I know it. Huge deal." Babble, babble, babble. She should have quit after "thanks."

He wasn't saying anything. That was the problem. If he'd said, "It's okay" or something she would have stopped babbling. But he merely watched her, his lips on the verge of a smile. On the verge. No smile. Important distinction.

Sara swallowed again, and attempted to end the conversation with some finesse. She linked her fingers together. "I wanted to reassure you that your trust in my competence has not been misplaced."

There. That should be precise enough for him.

"Right." He looked down at his desk. "Well, I'll just delete this scathing memo to the head of Human Resources denouncing your...competence."

He pressed a key on the open laptop on the desk in front of him and then closed it.

Sara forgot to breathe.

Simon smiled faintly. "I was joking."

"Oh!" Sara giggled inanely. "I knew that!"

"No, you didn't."

"No, I didn't."

"A lot of people don't get my jokes. I've always thought I was quite witty." The line was delivered with the perfect deadpan expression. Despite his straitlaced reputation, the man clearly had a sense of humor. *Don't think about that.*

Sara laughed, then wondered if she should have. "Maybe your jokes are just too subtle."

"Chalk it up to my repressed boarding school upbringing."

"In England?"

"Yes."

"You have a faint accent," she told him so he wouldn't think she'd been snooping in his file. And she hadn't—not much.

"So does anyone who isn't from Texas. I do try. I've

been sprinkling y'alls and howdys throughout all my conversations."

Sara tried to imagine a "y'all" passing Simon's lips. Which made her look at his lips and the way they rested in that almost-smile position. His square jaw made him look strong, but the lips gave him a hint of vulnerability. All in all, it was a potent combination, especially considering his other body parts, which Sara had in no way forgotten.

He had a way of looking at her—maybe everyone—which made her believe that his entire attention was focused on her.

That was potent, too. It kept her focused on him and not on the fact that she should leave and he was being too polite to shoo her out.

Politeness was a lost art these days and highly underrated, Sara thought. Was it on her list of preferred male traits?

Voices erupted from the elevator. Female voices. Surely they were coming to meet with Simon. "Your visitors are here, so I'll take off. Thanks again."

He looked as though he was going to say something when Sara distinctly heard the sound of running. She was so surprised that she didn't go anywhere. An instant later, two girls rounded the corner and headed straight for her. Sara stepped back into the office as the taller of the two reached out and slapped the door frame. "I won!"

"Kayla," Simon said sternly.

Sara stood there, filled with an entirely inappropriate curiosity.

"This is a place of business," he continued.

Kayla gave him a disgusted look. "Oh, chill."

He took a deep breath that told Sara he'd taken many deep breaths in regard to Kayla. He turned to the dark-haired girl beside Kayla. "Howdy, Amber. How're y'all doing?"

Sara tried to muffle her burst of surprised laughter and thought she was going to swallow her tongue. She made a noise that drew Kayla's attention.

"Hey, is this your girlfriend?" Kayla eyed her with Hayden-like interest.

Sara judged her to be about twelve or thirteen, the age when girls had boys on the brain. Unlike Sara who had men on the brain.

"I work with Mr. Northrup," she said.

"*Mr.* Northrup!" Kayla giggled and jostled a smiling Amber.

"Kayla, I told you girls not to run." A woman appeared in the doorway of Simon's office.

"Mom! It's after hours. Nobody cares."

Sara stared at Kayla's mother. The woman was sophisticated perfection and moved with supreme self-confidence. It was as though Missy and Hayden had merged. Merged their ages, too. She looked to be in her early thirties.

And it wasn't as though she was wearing a killer ladies-who-lunch suit, either. No, she had on slacks and pointy-toed shoes or boots, and a top with a matching sweater's sleeves tied around her neck just *so*. A leather messenger bag—Prada? Kate Spade?— was slung over her shoulder.

Here, before her, was the perfect woman, and Sara realized just how far she was going to have to go to attract and hold the interest of Simon Northrup's type.

Clearly, this was the woman and child that the rumor mill had been buzzing about. Well. Had she ever thought for one minute about flirting for real with Simon Northrup, this chance meeting put an end to that.

She was lucky. Oh, so lucky. She cringed at the thought of future humiliation averted.

There would be plenty of cringing and more humiliation at the complete and ruthless assessment of herself that would occur later, when she compared herself to the polished woman eyeing her with faintly dismissive curiosity. Oh, to master that look. Hayden no doubt had it in her arsenal. Sara would ask her to teach it to her.

Now if she could just slink away unnoticed....

"Sara?" Simon's voice stopped her.

He was going to introduce her. *No. Please don't. There'll be the inevitable comparisons and—*

But of course he would introduce her because he was *polite*. Maybe politeness was overrated after all.

"This wild thing is my half sister, Kayla, and this is her friend, Amber."

Sara nodded, gathering what poise she could. Plastering a smile to her face, she turned toward the woman who was probably Simon's lover. Someone who didn't have to jam a photocopier to see his—better not go there.

"And this is my stepmother, Joanna."

3

JOANNA WAS PISSED. Simon took a small pleasure in watching her face take on that set, slightly frowning look. She didn't like him to refer to her as his stepmother, but since she *was* his stepmother she couldn't object.

Simon knew the office grapevine would be humming with the information by tomorrow morning. Live by the grapevine, die by the grapevine. He knew people had wondered about Joanna and Kayla and had assumed he was dating. He'd allowed the rumor to grow because right now, Joanna and Kayla had first call on his time and emotional energy. Especially Kayla.

He hadn't fully understood the term "emotional energy" until recently or that it was something different from any other energy. But Kayla...Kayla needed something. Joanna needed something, too, but it wasn't up to Simon to provide it. Which was a good thing, since dealing with Kayla pretty much zapped him.

Date? Not likely. At this point, the best he could hope for was a mutually pleasurable physical encounter when he traveled on business. An encounter with a woman who also wanted no more than a night, or two.

A woman he wouldn't have to face at the office afterward.

So why hadn't he taken advantage of the last several opportunities? Why had he chosen room service and movies on cable instead?

Because he was at the stage in life where he wanted more. He wanted a meaningful relationship, though he'd be drummed out of the male gender if he ever said so aloud. But Simon wanted a family of his own, and he knew it. Unfortunately, he had to deal with the family he already had.

WHOA. BACK UP. Back the heck up. Stepmother? Simon's introduction of Kayla finally registered. Half sister. He'd said half sister. *Half sister?* And more importantly, *stepmother?*

Sara knew she should say something, maybe something like, "Pleased to meet you." But was she pleased? Was Simon pleased that he'd introduced her?

It's a polite response. It doesn't have to mean anything.

She turned to Simon, ready to mouth the polite response and make her escape. And call Hayden with some of the juiciest gossip that had ever come Sara's way.

"So where're we gonna eat?" Kayla asked before Sara could say anything.

"I have reservations at La Griglia."

Wow. Fancy. But not too fancy.

"Simon!" Joanna made a face. Kind of a classy annoyed face. Sara filed it away as another expression she'd like to acquire.

"The girls aren't dressed for La Griglia," Joanna continued.

No kidding. If those girls wore more than a yard of fabric between them, Sara would be surprised. She glanced at Simon, unable to help herself. She should have left by now, but truly she couldn't figure out a way to leave without attracting attention. Okay, she wasn't trying all that hard. It would take a saint to leave now.

Simon was looking at Kayla and Amber. Sara had been to La Griglia once. It was moderately expensive and Italian. Simon had got the Italian part right. Most everyone liked Italian food, but the atmosphere was chic and to-be-seen. Not the place to take children, though Kayla had just passed the point of childhood and was deep into burgeoning adolescence. In fact, she was about to burgeon right out of those shorts. Her short shorts and tank top definitely looked mall food-courtish, though the businessmen and fifty-somethings at La Griglia were bound to enjoy the view.

"What's wrong with the way we're dressed?" Kayla asked. "I think we look cute." She thrust her size zero hips to the side.

Enjoy them now, honey. If the freshman fifteen don't get you, take-out and weekend dates with Ben & Jerry's will.

Kayla was that fun age between child and woman. She was trying to figure out who she was and what she was going to do—not unlike Sara right at this minute.

Only Sara had had fifteen or so more years to figure it all out.

How depressing was that? Sara so needed to get out of Simon's office. She tried to catch his eye. He glanced at her at the exact moment she turned to him. He looked vulnerable and uncertain. Very un-Simon-like. Yeah, anything he said in response would probably be wrong. Sympathy kept her rooted to the spot.

"La Griglia is a nice restaurant," he said slowly. "Not a casual sort of place."

"That's the point," snipped Joanna.

Sara wanted to do something to Joanna. Maybe take her aside and smack her.

"Well, I'm going to have to get to class." Joanna gave Kayla and Amber a once-over before removing her sunglasses from the top of her head and putting them on. "I suppose they'll be okay." But the way she said it, everyone knew they wouldn't be okay.

What a nasty piece of work. Hayden would have put her in her place, but Sara was no Hayden.

Amber, who had been silent up until now, looked stricken.

Kayla looked disgusted. "Is it some stuffy place? I told you I didn't want to go to stuffy places anymore."

"It's one of the top-rated restaurants in Houston. I thought it would be a treat," Simon said quietly.

Awwww, Sara thought and sent a vicious and completely unnoticed look at Joanna. Why didn't she say something parental like "Mind your manners?"

"Can we take a limo?" Kayla asked.

"I was planning to drive."

"Man." Kayla wore a sullen expression.

"Limos are for entertaining clients," Simon said in the voice of one who knows he's doomed. "You don't like going out with clients."

Joanna bailed. "I've got a seven o'clock class." She waggled her fingers, wrinkled her nose at Sara and left.

Simon looked at Sara. If ever there was a cry for help, this was it. And Sara responded to the call. Willingly. Gladly.

"They really aren't dressed for La Griglia," she said as though she'd been there many times herself. "You know what they'd like? Dave and Busters."

"Dave and Busters!" Kayla's whole demeanor changed.

"I love that place," Amber said. "But since you have to be with an adult, I don't get to go there unless it's a special occasion, or something. My cousin's graduation was the last time I got to go there. I still have leftover tickets." She groaned. "But I didn't bring them with me."

"Tickets?" asked Simon.

He looked lost. Appealingly lost. The kind of lost where Sara could be the rescuer. Now here was a nice switch on the traditional fantasy. Sara liked it. Now *she* could appear competent in front of *him*.

And she owed him big time. Huge time. She could have been fired. Clearly, he wanted to make good with his sister, so Sara would help him. Just as clearly, but unbelievably, he didn't know about Dave and Buster's.

Sara would cover for him because it was very uncool not to know about Dave and Buster's.

"I love Dave and Buster's," she said. "There's nothing like it for relieving stress. I mean, sometimes I just want to chill out and play pool, but other times, I can't wait to get in one of those pods and blow people up."

"Yeah!" Kayla and Amber clutched each other as they looked from Simon to Sara and back. Kayla's eyes were as dark as her big brother's and just as intense.

"The drinks aren't bad, either, are they, Simon?" Sara grinned at him.

And he grinned back. Oh, boy. Talk about fuel for her crush.

"You're right," he said. "I am more in a Dave and Buster's mood. Would you like to come with us?"

Sara had half anticipated the invitation. Still...Simon Northrup. Could she? Should she?

"We're going to Dave and Buster's? For real?" Kayla looked stunned. Amber looked impressed. And Simon, well, Simon managed to look sexy and grateful at the same time.

To Sara's surprise, Kayla grabbed her arm. "You're gonna come with us, right?" She looked from Sara to Simon and back. "I mean, Dave and Buster's...you've gotta be cool."

Sara laughed, knowing exactly what Kayla was thinking—here was somebody to baby-sit big brother while she and Amber played video games. "Sure, I'll go."

Kayla and Amber jumped up and down and squealed.

"Reservations?" Simon asked Sara beneath the noise.

She shook her head. "We just head on out."

Simon grabbed his jacket and turned out the lights. As the girls galloped down the hall, he looked at Sara. "You can do this? It's not interfering with any other plans?"

"You think I'd abandon you now?"

He winced. "Am I that transparently desperate?"

"Oh, yeah."

He laughed. "Thank you for the lifeline."

"Just tossing back the one you threw me earlier."

The look he gave her was…was something. Was it interest? In her? No, there wasn't a gleam. Hayden and Missy said she'd see a gleam. She wanted to see that gleam, which meant she'd probably spend the whole evening trying to cause one.

She drove her own car, leading the way so Simon wouldn't have to admit that he didn't know where Dave and Buster's was. His car was a plush luxomobile, on the sedate side for her, but she knew he had to drive visitors around. Besides, on her list hadn't she only specified that her perfect man's car should be running?

When they arrived at the restaurant, Amber and Kayla fled to the bathroom to put on lip gloss and eye makeup, Sara guessed.

Simon gripped her arm. "Quick—what kind of place is this?"

Sara briefed him. "Video games. Pinball machines. Super interactive games that you can play against other people by getting in pods."

"Pods, got it."

"Expensive."

"Roger that."

"You can win tickets that are redeemable for prizes. Mostly plastic junk, but some cool stuff. To eat, there's pizza and hamburgers and drinks, but regular adult meals, if you want them. It's a lot of fun." When he nodded in all seriousness, she added, "It's not a place to be uptight."

Simon immediately removed his tie and stuffed it into his pocket. He sure got points for catching on quick. If he stuck with Sara, Kayla would think he was the coolest big brother ever.

Sara smiled, just because he was trying so hard.

Simon smiled back.

Oh, yes. The smile was good. The smile drew a person—her—right in. The smile made a person—her, again—forget other stuff, stuff like time and place and circumstances.

Sara reached out, then hesitated.

"What?" Simon asked.

"Uh...you need to..." She hesitantly unbuttoned the top button of his shirt.

She could feel the warmth of his skin and was aware that his eyes never left her face. When she glanced up at him, she saw an intensity in his expression, but she wasn't sure what it conveyed. It was an expression she wasn't familiar with and she tried to analyze it. She wanted to be able to report back to Hayden and Missy and see what their take was.

Without knowing better, she'd say it was longing. But why would Simon Northrup look longingly at her?

The girls erupted from the restrooms and Sara took a step backward. They'd been hitting the lip gloss and some flowery scent and had combed their hair. Their cheeks and eyes sparkled—and not just from excitement.

Simon either didn't notice, or wisely chose not to say anything.

Kayla gave Sara a wary look and Sara responded by brushing one of her own cheeks to indicate that Kayla had gone too heavy on the glitter. Kayla rubbed at her cheek and raised her eyebrows. Sara gave her a nod and a discreet thumbs-up. Too bad Sara only had a big brother. She would have been a really cool big sister.

They were shown to a table and Sara made sure they ordered pizza. Kayla would have glowed, Sara thought, even without the glittery skin gel.

"This rocks!" She and Amber craned their necks all around.

"While we wait for the pizza, I bet Kayla and Amber would like to play some games," Sara prompted.

Kayla quivered in delight.

Simon looked at her. "It's fine with me."

Sara raised her eyebrows. "Now, Simon, don't tease.

Go ahead and give them some token money." She looked at Kayla. "He's afraid you'll forget about the pizza and we'll be stuck here with a bunch of cold cheese."

"No, we won't. Promise!"

Simon reached into his pocket for change. "Let's see what I've got here." He meticulously picked out five quarters.

"You are such a kidder." Sara hoped he actually was kidding. With him, it was hard to tell. "Give me that wallet, bud." The girls giggled as Sara snatched it out of his unresisting hands and looked through the folding money. Okay, so his walking around money equaled her next month's rent. Wasn't financial solvency on her ideal-man list?

She shouldn't be thinking of Simon in terms of the list and drat Hayden for suggesting him.

She pulled out a twenty and nudged Simon's foot when he opened his mouth to object. "Get a couple of power cards and come back for the pizza, or we'll come find you. And you know how embarrassing *that* would be."

Kayla snatched the twenty and she and Amber hurried off with a gushing thanks, a giggle and two huge smiles.

Simon stared after them. "You gave her twenty dollars."

"And you'll give her twenty more before the night is over. Expensive, but a bargain. Did you see her face?"

"Yes." He looked at Sara. A long time. Long enough for her insides to get fluttery. "Thanks."

"I owed you," she told him.

"Not this much."

"More."

"I'd argue, but the night is very young and Kayla is very temperamental."

"Hormones. Don't worry about it."

"Never underestimate the power of hormones."

Good advice, because Sara was aware of a little hormone simmering herself. They needed to just unsimmer because number one, while she didn't actually work with, or for, Simon, they did work at the same company and anyone who had ever read *Cosmo* knew that was a royal no-no. Sara even had the added reinforcement of Hayden's example. Examples. Hayden survived just fine, though, because when she was finished with men—and she was usually finished with them first—she was finished. Completely. There were sticky moments from those who failed to get the message, but they all eventually got said message because Hayden could be witheringly blunt.

Sara didn't ever seem to be finished with men before they were finished with her. She also had a low humiliation threshold. That would be the number two reason to cool it with Simon.

Very mature and rational reasoning on why this "date" was purely for practice, if Sara did say so herself, conveniently ignoring the fact that she'd decided not to practice on Simon. She waited for the coolness and calmness of logic to soothe the prickly awareness of him. The awareness part wasn't bad; it added a nice, harmless zing to their dealings.

It was the prickles. Sara imagined hormones jumping just beneath her skin. Prickles weren't good. Prickles generally led past awareness right into touching. Then more touching...and stroking...and kissing...and your-place-or-mine-ing...and looking for the blinking light on the answering machine...and avoiding him at work.

No. Not this time. Not until there was a chance of reciprocity. She'd add that to the list and make sure Missy put it in the spreadsheet. In the meantime, a prickly Sara drank deeply from her glass of iced water in hopes of drowning the little suckers.

"You're probably wondering about Kayla," Simon said out of nowhere.

Sara nearly choked. "Not really."

He just looked at her.

"Okay." Carefully, she set down her glass. "Yes. But I'm too polite to ask."

Simon gave her a half smile. It was a quick gesture, but, oh, it really tugged the heart strings. A tugged heart string was much more lethal than mere prickles. How could he do that? By revealing that he was vulnerable, that's how. Strong men with a hint of vulnerability were just so darn irresistible.

"I dated Joanna in college."

Sara had a feeling she didn't want to hear this.

"I took her home one Christmas to meet my parents."

Nope. She definitely didn't want to hear this.

He drew a deep breath, then another.

Sara couldn't stand it. "You don't have to—"

He held up a hand and fired a barrage of staccatolike information at her. "My father fell for her. Instantly. It destroyed my parents' marriage. They divorced when Joanna got pregnant with Kayla. She and my father married. I never saw them again until he was dying."

Men just did *not* know how to tell a story. If such a betrayal had happened to her, it would have been good for at least an hour in the telling and a whole evening devoted to exploring motivations and feelings, along with emotional nurturing and revenge plotting. There would certainly be chocolate involved and probably alcohol as well.

Because he was a man, Simon had no doubt buried all his hurt and betrayal. It wasn't healthy. Women were much healthier in that respect, even with all the alcohol and chocolate.

"I went back for a 'deathbed reconciliation.'" He made air quotes with his fingers. "He asked me to look after Joanna and Kayla. I thought what bloody nerve— Joanna could look after herself. But there was Kayla." Simon looked down at his hands that he'd laced around his own water glass. "She was my sister. You have to understand that I hadn't ever thought about her that way. She was just Joanna's baby. Anyway, after my father died, Joanna and Kayla moved to Houston because Joanna wants to finish her degree and because I'm here to help with Kayla.''

Sara was trying not to be judgmental about Joanna. And failing.

''Kayla is something else. She sasses her mother and Joanna isn't firm enough with her. She's getting away with who knows what. It's not hard to see that she was spoiled. I don't have any other brothers or sisters, so there weren't any grandkids for my father to indulge.''

Sara filed that tidbit away.

''If someone doesn't take her in hand, this little girl is headed for trouble. Amber isn't a problem. In fact, if I were Amber's father, I wouldn't want her to associate with Kayla, but I'm not Amber's father. And I'm not Kayla's father. Nevertheless, Joanna wants me to help with her and I think it's a good idea.''

Sara had a feeling that wasn't all Joanna wanted.

Simon spread his hands. ''Not only have I not had experience with teenage girls since I was a teenage boy, I never even met Kayla until she was ten years old. Do you think that's horrible?''

Surprised he asked, Sara quickly shook her head. ''I have no right to judge you.''

''Which means you have.''

''Not really. I would have been mad, too. And I admire you for trying to make things right with her now.''

''I don't know. I'm having trouble getting past the fact that she's more than twenty years younger than I am—and had I not brought Joanna home that Christmas...I've had to deal with a lot of bitterness. And I did." He smiled. "I'm still dealing with the guilt over ignoring Kayla, though."

Okay. This guy had serious baggage. Number one on her no way, José list. If he couldn't be there for her one hundred percent, it didn't matter how great he was otherwise. "Look," she said. "We don't know each other very well. I don't want you to feel awkward for telling me all this stuff." She brightened her voice. "I suggest a pitcher of margaritas. What do you say?"

He gave her a wry look. "I think you're a wise woman."

"Yeah, and I saw that wallet. You have enough cash to keep those two busy for hours. And, hey, there's a lot of great games you'd find fun, too."

Simon grinned. He suddenly looked like a college kid. Impulsively, Sara asked, "How old are you?"

"Thirty-three."

Sara dropped her jaw. Ten years younger than she would have guessed. Okay, maybe not ten, but he'd said he was more than twenty years older than Kayla and it seemed to fit.

"Don't give me that look."

"What look?"

Simon flagged down their waiter and ordered the margaritas. "You know what look."

She did. "Well, you just act older."

"Just because I don't participate in casual Fridays..."

"And why don't you?"

"Because I constantly deal with European clients.

They don't do casual Fridays. I'm dressing for them. Besides, I'm more comfortable in suits. Women should wear suits all the time," he told her. "Trust me when I tell you that casual Fridays are no friend of women in the workplace."

He grinned and shook his head. "I can't believe I'm giving fashion advice."

"And I can't believe I'm taking it."

Their pizza and margaritas arrived just then, which was good because Sara wanted a margarita about now.

"I never drank these until I moved here," Simon said.

"They are the national drink of Texas." Sara held up her glass and they clinked the salty rims together.

As he drank, Simon looked around for the girls.

"They'll be at the midway." Sara nodded to the garish archway leading from the room. "It's on the other side of the building."

"Great." He stared down at the huge pizza.

"Have a slice." Taking one for herself, Sara tilted it so the pepperoni grease could run off.

"And you're eating that why...?"

He'd caught her just as she took a mouthful. She held up a finger as she chewed and swallowed. "Because it tastes fabulous." She nudged the plate toward him. "Do not try to pretend you've never eaten pizza."

"Not one so enthusiastically greasy."

"You must not order pepperoni, then. Pepperoni *is* grease. And salt, too. Yummy, yummy."

"I get portabella, green pepper and sliced tomatoes with Parmesan shavings grilled over a wood fire."

"Oh, you poor, poor, deprived man." She picked up a piece. "Eat."

"But the girls—"

"Will come back when they run out of money. Not too much longer, I think."

Holding her gaze with his, Simon opened his mouth and Sara moved the pizza toward him. After chewing a mouthful, he raised his eyebrows and nodded. "I'll admit that it has a certain gooey charm that a grilled portabella mushroom lacks."

"I guess so."

He looked around again and Sara realized he was worried about the girls. She wasn't because she'd been watching the exit and the midway video monitors behind him. "Does Kayla have a pager or a cell phone?"

"Good idea." He reached for his and punched a single number.

So he had his little sister's cell number on autodial.

"Pizza's here," he said into the phone and closed it.

Sara was eating said pizza and enjoying it thoroughly. Maybe too thoroughly because she was aware of Simon doing his staring thing again. Just observing her. It made her self-conscious, especially when a string of cheese caught on her chin. Why wasn't he eating? She set the slice down and pointed to his. "Aren't you going to eat?"

"I enjoy watching you eat. You're really into it."

Pig woman. What an attractive image. "You can't do that—not without eating, too. It's too weird."

He laughed and picked up his pizza.

She was liking him a little too much, here.

"So, what's between you and Joanna?" That should be a mood killer.

"Nothing." He calmly bit into his pizza.

"Does she want there to be something?"

"I don't know. I don't care."

Sara believed him. It would have been more helpful if she didn't.

Simon was in an alien land. If Kayla had been a boy, he would have had a frame of reference, but Kayla was almost a teenage girl. He'd thought a nice grown-up restaurant like La Griglia would be a treat. Obviously not.

If Sara hadn't been in his office, he would have experienced yet another failure with his sister. But now, watching as she and Amber galloped to their table, their smiles huge, he realized it was the first time he'd ever seen Kayla completely happy when she was with him.

She and Amber grabbed pieces of pizza and he started to correct them, or at least Kayla, but didn't and was rewarded by hearing them tell about the games they'd played. The words tumbled out of them. They looked at him a couple of times and he made all the right noises, he thought.

Sara picked up two plastic cards that looked like credit cards. "They need their power cards recharged."

"After pizza?" he asked.

Sara grinned at him. She had a small, well-shaped mouth and a cute indentation at the corner when she smiled. It distracted him from immediately noticing that she was gesturing downward with the power cards.

The pizza was gone. "Did you two inhale it?"

They giggled.

"Do you want more?"

They shook their heads. Sara took a card in each hand and waved them back and forth as though signaling.

"I take it me and my wallet are invited to the midway." This caused more giggling, some from Sara.

As he followed them across the restaurant toward the midway arch, Simon felt as though he'd had a breakthrough with Kayla. The relief was enormous. His little sister apparently harbored a huge resentment because she felt he'd ignored her. Simon knew he had Joanna to thank for making her feel that way.

But he also accepted the blame because he'd never actually thought of her as his sister. He hadn't thought of her at all, really. He'd been so hurt and the situation had been so awkward, that he'd stayed away. Now he was struggling to get to know this girl who shared a father with him and tonight's success was entirely due to Sara.

Sara. One minute, he'd been up to his elbows in the copier and the next, he'd looked over his shoulder at her standing there and felt his heart skip a beat. And just like that, he was back in the game. Oh, he had the best of intentions with regard to Kayla, but in his mind, Simon had already traveled from a chance meeting at a photocopier to rethinking his No Women rule. And rethinking it with Sara.

Simon looked at her standing in line, laughing and talking about video games to the girls with a casual ease that he envied. If she had any idea of what he was thinking, she'd run. Because he wanted to touch her. Curl his hand around her nape, draw her close and kiss her. Right here. Right now. He wanted to taste her. Devour her.

Instead, he extravagantly shoved bills at the cashier, endured squeals and hugs from both Kayla *and* Amber, then smiled at Sara. "Come on." He nodded toward a row of white pods. "Let's go kill some aliens."

4

THE NEXT DAY, Sara immediately set up another lunch with Missy and Hayden in the atrium café of their building.

She spotted them from the top of the escalator and could tell they were arguing. It was to be expected, since they usually rationed the time spent in each other's company, and two lunches in two days was pushing it.

Tra la la, Sara didn't care. She swung by the salad bar for a Chinese chicken salad and a blueberry cornbread muffin, then headed toward the table, secure in the knowledge that she was about to drop a gossip bomb. Simon hadn't asked her to keep it secret, so it was detonation in five minutes.

Hayden was looking fierce, but trying not to frown. Hayden wouldn't waste wrinkle-inducing frowns on women.

Missy had brought charts and printed spreadsheets.

"...higher probability," Missy was saying.

"I'm not arguing that point," Hayden argued. "I'm arguing about showing up dressed as June Cleaver."

"The Beaver's mother was a lady of refinement."

"Who needed a man who could ruffle those petti-coats. And I'm sorry, but ole Ward—"

"Greetings all." Sara slid onto a chair and popped the plastic top off her salad. "Simon Northrup and I went out for dinner last night."

Boom. And suddenly, the only sound was Sara crunching the water chestnuts from her salad.

She savored the moment. The chicken salad was pretty good, too. And the best was yet to come. Missy, a temp who floated from department to department, always knew any gossip worth knowing, and Hayden had an uncanny ability to predict gossip before it happened; Sara rarely—actually, never—got to surprise them.

And they were surprised now. Shocked. Stunned. It wasn't very flattering, if she thought about it, but she wasn't going to think about it. She told them about Simon, his sister and his stepmother. She may have lingered on the stepmother a little.

Hayden forgot herself so much as to drop her jaw. Missy's eyes were so wide, her eyebrows disappeared beneath her bangs.

It was a great moment. One of the highlights of Sara's life, which was pretty pitiful.

"You're kidding," Hayden finally said.

"She can't be kidding," Missy said. "She's not capable of making up something that good."

"Hey," Sara protested mildly. She could be gracious in victory.

"So he *is* available," Hayden mused.

"Hayden!" Missy cut her eyes toward Sara.

"Oh." Hayden snapped back from whatever seductive fantasy she'd been weaving. "Sara, of course I'll defer to you."

It bugged her the way she said it, as though Sara couldn't hold her own against Hayden should Hayden decide to go after Simon.

What was she thinking? No way could she hold her own against Hayden. Sara stopped short of staking her claim, though it was a wrenching decision, especially when she kept mentally replaying highlights from yesterday. The photocopier session was a favorite, but so was Simon laughing and laughing while they battled aliens together. His eyes crinkled in a way that she particularly liked and he had a habit of steering her through crowds by casually touching her arm, or resting his hand in the small of her back. She had begun to anticipate his touch and deliberately jostled against him at the video games.

It took one extra stumble—a happy accident—and Simon's arms shooting out to steady her and she wasn't steady at all. His face was close to hers and when he leaned down, she knew, just knew, he was going to kiss her. And she was all for that. She'd even closed her eyes, but all he did was speak close to her ear so he could be heard above the noise, "Are you all right?"

She would have been better if he'd kissed her, but she'd nodded, and tried to remember why Simon wasn't right for her.

She was reminded by Kayla and her little shadow, Amber, who interrupted them about nine hundred times. Really. Kept them constantly informed of the latest ticket count. Begged them to play machines that spit out the red strings. Squealed a lot. Simon would respond instantly, even in midsentence. He'd even walked away from Sara during a game. Not good.

Sara might as well let Hayden have him, because Hayden wouldn't put up with that for a minute. Actually, Hayden wouldn't last a minute with Simon, but Sara wasn't going to tell her that.

Still, even though Simon was wrong for her, Sara hated the idea of Hayden going after him. Really hated it. Except the thought of Hayden steamrolling over Joanna was nice. But was the world ready for a Kayla who'd been influenced by Hayden? "I don't think he's exactly available," was what she finally said to Hayden.

"You said he wasn't dating anyone."

Had she said that?

"He's dating Sara," Missy maintained. "They had dinner last night."

"In a pinball palace with his kid sister." Hayden dismissed what had been a fun evening for Sara. "That wasn't a date. Sara was a baby-sitter."

"She was not!" Missy hotly defended her. "They drank margaritas. You don't drink margaritas with your baby-sitter."

"Has he called her?" They both looked at Sara.

"Uh..."

"Give it some time," Missy said.

Great. Now she was going to go home and check for a blinking light on her answering machine.

Except she hadn't given Simon her telephone number.

And he hadn't asked.

She sighed. Why was it that she always ended up wanting men who didn't want her or were bad for her? And they'd had what would have been a perfect first date, too, if it had been a real date. Which it hadn't been.

"Never mind that." Missy dragged her spreadsheet across the table. She wrote in Simon's name and went across the columns where she'd listed all the attributes Sara had mentioned she wanted.

Sara watched as Missy checked off a whole lot of good qualities for Simon Northrup. He almost had a perfect score, darn it.

"He has issues," she said in a quiet voice.

"What issues?" Missy asked.

"Oh, hon, the sister and the beautiful, but evil, step-mother, of course," Hayden said in a bored tone.

"He said his top priority was establishing a relation-ship with his sister and being a solid influence in her life," Sara recited.

"Issue with a capital *I*." Hayden pointed to the col-umn, which Missy had printed in red, that featured Sara's number-one required trait—total devotion. "That's the deal breaker." Hayden didn't sound too broken up about it.

"Is it, Sara?"

With the last lingering memories of Simon fixing the copier, smiling down at her, touching her back and just plain looking at her dancing in her head, Sara forced herself to nod. It was a deal breaker. It had to be.

Missy slumped, a lapse in posture that indicated her extreme disappointment. As they all watched, she slowly drew a line through Simon's name and extended it all the way across the page.

"All righty then. Onward with the search." Hayden's voice was suspiciously cheerful.

Sara wondered if she should warn Simon.

Missy placed a chart on top of the spreadsheet. "It's lucky for you that I'm spending a couple of weeks in the travel department. I asked around and gathered data on restaurants and hotels frequented by businessmen fitting your search parameters."

"Let me see that." Hayden looked over Missy's chart and tossed it back. "Those are stuffy places. Old married men stay there."

"Men accustomed to a certain quality of life supported by a mid-six figure income before stock options and bonuses stay there. And if they're married, there is a good chance that they'll have a son in medical school, law school or grad school."

"So Sara will be saddled with a husband with thousands in school loans to repay? I don't see how this will improve her quality of life."

Neither did Sara, but she merely crunched her salad and listened to the two of them.

"Even if the son is a little young, he won't always be in debt."

"Hmm." Hayden was looking off into space, her high-heeled foot swinging.

"The other kind of man Sara would meet would be a go-getter who's deliberately courting the establishment by staying in a conservative old-money kind of place. He's Sara's best bet because he'll be desperate—"

"Hey!"

"—for the company of somebody his own age after spending all day deferring to his elders."

There was silence. Sara had picked out all the water chestnuts. She looked at Hayden.

Hayden lifted her shoulder, her foot still swinging.

Missy took that as agreement. "Which is why Sara should dress with understated class. Remember, our target wants to fit in with old money. Sara will be demonstrating that she's at home with that lifestyle."

"She can be classy, but she's going to have to be sexy classy, or she won't attract anyone's attention."

"We don't want her to attract attention, we want her to pique interest. I suggest we meet for drinks tomorrow night at the Stratford Oaks downtown. Sara, you'll need a good leather briefcase or portfolio, a suit, some pearls—"

"Oh, please! Why not just have her go around curtsying to everyone!"

"Money attracts money!" Missy snapped. "At the

very least, you'll need expensive shoes, Sara. After work, go invest in some black designer pumps."

"Only gay men know designers," Hayden scoffed.

"These men will know quality." Missy's gaze flicked toward Hayden's shoes. "Buy one get one free at the Shoe Barn?"

Hayden looked Missy up and down. "A garage sale at the convent?"

"Okay. Time-out." Neither Missy nor Hayden looked at Sara. "It's agreed that we'll meet at the Stratford Oaks downtown after work tomorrow. I'll buy new shoes. And a Wonderbra."

"You don't already have one?" both Missy and Hayden asked in unison.

"Well, now," Hayden said with a look at Missy.

"It improves the fit of some of my dresses." Missy gathered up the papers. "I have to scoot, y'all. Phone calls," she explained. "Tootles."

Hayden waited until she was out of earshot. "Okay, listen up, Sara. You can take Miss Prissy Missy's advice about where to meet men, but for attracting them, you listen to me. Do you really want to attract a man who is turned on by pearls and a buttoned-up collar? Can you imagine him in bed? We're talking twin beds here. We're talking a man with a Madonna complex. Once you're his wife and especially after the kids, say goodbye to fun in the sack. What Missy didn't mention is that those guys are the ones who keep mistresses."

She seemed to know what she was talking about. "Hayden, have you...?"

"Not knowingly. I mean, when I was young and stupid, I kinda sorta was. But I didn't know it."

"Huh?"

"Well, he was older and richer and I was younger and poorer and I enjoyed the places he took me and when he said that he owned some apartments and some were just sitting empty and I'd be doing him a favor by keeping one occupied and I could save rent, too, well…" She gave Sara a what's-a-girl-gonna-do look.

"So how long did it last?"

Hayden gave a crack of laughter. "Not very long. I didn't understand the whole mistress concept and I had a guy over. The old man walked in on us! He didn't knock or anything. In fact I had no idea he expected me to hang around and be available for his visits and only his visits." She laughed again. "I was sooo naive."

Sara pondered the image of a naive Hayden. Nope. Couldn't manage it.

Hayden stood. "So tomorrow night, I want to see you in a slit skirt and a Wonderbra. Don't let me down."

SARA'S FEET were killing her. She was wearing three hundred dollar shoes. And that was three hundred dollars *on sale*. Three hundred dollar shoes weren't supposed to hurt, were they?

They sure looked good. High-heeled black pumps that ought to please Missy. An impressive amount of manufactured cleavage to please Hayden. A new black skirt with a fairly high slit, also to please Hayden because frankly, she had made a lot of sense with that twin bed comment.

The bar of the Stratford Oaks Hotel looked—and smelled—like the inside of an English men's club. Yeah, old money would feel right at home with all the old leather, and the old cigar smoke.

Hayden was already there. No one could miss Hayden, who was defiantly dressed in a tight, low-cut red dress. She sat at the bar with her legs crossed as she read a newspaper. Two clusters of men tried to pretend they weren't watching her, but since they'd all moved their chairs so that no one had his back to her, they weren't fooling anybody.

Missy was there, too, but Sara hadn't seen her at first. Missy clearly didn't want anything to do with Hayden. She had her Palm Pilot out and her hair twisted up with some curls loose, wore black glasses and yes, there were the pearls, a black skirt and white blouse and black shoes.

Okay, this was a no-win situation. Who was she supposed to sit with?

"Sara!" Hayden waved at her from the bar. The men swiveled their heads to look at Sara.

Okay. Hayden it was. Missy shuddered and turned a shoulder toward Hayden as she gave a warning look to Sara. Sara stuck her leg out as she passed. "Check out the shoes."

"Very nice," Missy said.

Personally, Sara thought that three hundred dollars deserved more than "very nice."

"Go sit next to Hayden. You'll look good by comparison."

Sara shook her head and tried not to limp as she made her way past low tables surrounded by dark green and luggage brown leather club chairs.

"Nice walk," Hayden commented. "Unbutton a button."

"I've already unbuttoned a button!"

"Unbutton another one." Hayden was checking out Sara's skirt. "What's with the granny gown?"

"Okay, it may be long, but it's got a big slit!" Sara moved her leg.

"Well, yeah, there's so much fabric to slit through. Hop up."

Sara eyed the swivel club chair at the bar and tested the give in her skirt. Not much. "How?"

"First turn so that the old guys can get a good view, then hitch up your skirt."

Sara decided not to hitch and discovered that her towering heels did help.

Hayden signaled the bartender, who took his time responding. "Your choices are gin and tonic, a real martini or Scotch on the rocks."

"That's all they've got?"

"That's what Missy says to order. She's got some chart linking male personalities and their drinks."

It figured. "A martini, I guess. Finding the right kind of man is a lot more complicated than I thought."

"No, honey, it's not." Hayden picked up her drink and casually crossed her legs the other way. She flipped back her hair and swiveled her chair, sending a long look at the men clustered several tables away.

They all stared down at their drinks.

"I don't want *those* men," Sara whispered.

"It was just practice." Hayden looked at her as she drank her martini. "Hon, you need a little oomph."

Sara looked at herself. "I feel very oomphy."

"Powder room. Now." Hayden slid off the bar seat.

Sara tried sliding, but caught her heel, so her exit was more of a lurch.

"Be right back." Hayden winked at the bartender.

He nodded as he wiped some glasses and set them up in twinkling rows on the mirrored back counter.

"See that? He's expecting more customers," Hayden murmured.

Once in the restroom, which was unexpectedly plush—in fact, Sara was sorry she couldn't hang out there—Hayden worked on Sarah's hair, then on her face.

Looking in the mirror, Sara grimaced. "I know you despise my usual muted neutrals but this look…"

"Smoky eyes."

"It's a little much, don't you think?"

"In here, yes, but that bar is so dark, you need a little extra."

"What's my hair's excuse?"

"Clipping it back on one side is very sultry. You should have used hot rollers."

"Hmm." Sara headed for the door.

"Sara—button."

"No."

"Then adjust." Hayden wiggled and hefted her breasts forward.

Frankly, Sara didn't have all that much to move around, but she'd forgotten about the wonders of the Wonderbra. She mimicked Hayden and was shocked at her new profile. "Now I know why it's called a Wonderbra—'cause you wonder where all this comes from." She looked down at herself. "I swear I see some thigh in there."

Hayden laughed. "Come on."

When they returned to the bar, it was to find that Missy had two yuppie-types sitting in her little conversation group.

"Should I go over there?" Sara asked uncertainly.

"Do you want to meet either of those two men?"

Did she? One was blond, the other light-brown-haired and Sara seemed to be on a dark-haired kick.

Simon Northrup had dark hair. Well, Simon Northrup wasn't here, was he? And she was and so were her two loyal friends who had given up their time to help Sara find a man. She needed to concentrate and quit whining about what she couldn't have.

With renewed determination, Sara hitched her skirt, climbed onto the barstool and flipped her hair. The bartender set her drink in front of her and exchanged Hayden's glass for a fresh one.

"Did you order that?" Sara asked.

"Not exactly." Hayden looked around, but no one came forward to claim her attention. "I guess there's a minimum if you sit at the bar." She raised the glass toward the unsmiling bartender. "I just don't intend to pay for my own drinks." She sipped her drink. "Now, what have we got?"

Men and a few women, but mostly men trickled into the bar area. Sara kept waiting for someone to approach them, but no one did.

Missy, on the other hand, had exchanged her yuppies for three older men. She was laughing and smiling and generally holding court.

Sara munched on her olive and dropped the toothpick in her now-empty glass. "Well, this sure is fun."

"Work must have sucked the testosterone right out of these men," Hayden said grimly.

"Maybe we should go sit at a table."

"Stay right there," Hayden ordered. "No Miss Priss is going to out-attract me!"

Hayden slithered down from the bar and headed toward a group of men, a little louder and a little younger than the others, who'd just come in. Clearly, they'd been attending some all-day seminar, because they were still wearing badges helpfully supplying their names.

Sara had planned to stay at the bar and watch, but at the last minute, Hayden reached out and practically pulled her along with her. Sara gritted her teeth behind her smile. She was not a mingler. She was more of a wait-for-them-to-come-to-her type. Only they never did.

"Y'all from out of town?" Hayden asked brightly, but not as brightly as her dress.

The two men nearest Hayden glanced at her, and then at each other. Hayden peered at their badges. "Hi, George from Pensacola and John from Dallas. Why, Dallas is just up the road. That makes us neighbors." She laughed. They didn't. Undeterred, she continued, "I'm Hayden and this is my friend Sara."

Sara smiled widely to overcome the I'd-like-to-be-anywhere-else feeling currently residing in her stomach. Or was her Wonderbra too tight? Either way, she didn't want to talk to George from Pensacola or John from Dallas. It looked like they didn't want to talk to her, either.

Hayden caught that. "Well, welcome to Houston, y'all. Hope you have a good time." She nudged Sara away.

"Okay, that's it," Sara muttered as they walked toward more convention attendees. "This is not working."

"That was just a warm-up. Look at all these lovely men." Hayden happily gestured around them. "I'll give Missy points for finding prime hunting ground." She looked at Sara. "Sara, for pity's sake, smile! Now, let's mingle."

It was definitely a one-sided mingle, Sara thought. The more resistance Hayden got from the men, the louder she laughed and the bigger her gestures became. At one point, she took a sip from a man's drink and gave him a wink. When she tried to give his glass back, he declined and moved away.

On the other side of the room, Missy was surrounded. Sara tried to slink over her way, but Hayden steered Sara toward the restrooms.

"I can't figure it out," Hayden said. "What's wrong with these men?"

"They know prostitution is illegal in the state of Texas." The bartender was waiting for them in the corridor leading to the restrooms, and cutting off their way.

"I beg your pardon!" Hayden gave him the kind of look that usually had men knocking back a shot of tequila to numb the effect.

"I don't want any trouble." The unsmiling bartender crossed his arms over his massive chest.

"Good, because we don't either." Hayden pushed open the women's restroom door.

The bartender stopped her. "Ma'am, I'm going to have to ask you to leave the premises."

"What?"

Sara had never seen Hayden completely flabbergasted before.

"You and your friend need to leave now."

"Well, I—is this about the drinks? You didn't give us a chance to pay for them!"

"Drinks are on the house, ma'am."

Hayden smiled. This was familiar territory for her. "They usually are."

Drinks weren't usually free for Sara, and Hayden's self-satisfied expression triggered a mental recap of their conversation and recent actions. And then she filtered it through the bartender's eyes. And then she understood. And wished she didn't.

"Come out the back, please."

"Oh, no. This—"

"Hayden." Sara swallowed dryly. "He thinks we're...working girls."

"Well, we are."

"Not that kind. Prostitutes."

"He does not!" But one look at the bartender's face and she gasped in outrage. "I demand an apology!"

"Are either of you registered at this hotel?"

"No, but—"

"Out the back."

He took hold of Hayden's arm as she tried to jerk it away. "Let me go! I demand to speak to the manager. How dare you! Is this the way you treat unescorted women? I'll report you to the Better Business Bureau and the Houston Convention and Visitors Bureau. And...and...that group that fights for women's rights. This is the twenty-first century! I can't believe that a woman in this day and age—"

The bartender set Hayden out the emergency fire exit. Sara followed meekly behind her. The heavy door banged shut.

Hayden paced in front of it. "I don't believe this. Do you know what just happened?"

"Yes. We were mistaken for hookers." Sara

squashed down her hair and buttoned her blouse all the way to the neck, but the top button kept slipping out, probably due to the strain of all her new cleavage, so she finally just left it undone.

Hayden gave her an anguished look. "Do I look like a hooker?"

"Not a cheap one," Sara said.

Hayden's expression changed. "You're jealous."

"No, I'm embarrassed and my feet hurt." They started walking and Sara pointed to the convention center down the street. "We're in a hotel bar near the convention center and we're trying to pick up men. Can you blame the guy?"

"Yes," Hayden snapped. "Where are we going?"

"I don't know about you, but I'm going back to tell Missy where we are."

Hayden narrowed her eyes. "I will never set foot in the Stratford Oaks again. Furthermore, I will see to it that no client of mine is ever booked at the Stratford Oaks. And I will put out the word to my colleagues that *they* shouldn't book anyone in the Stratford Oaks." They reached the street entrance of the parking garage. "This is where we part company."

Fine with her. Sara figured she shouldn't have any trouble getting back into the bar unaccompanied by Hayden in the tight red dress. "Okay, I'll tell Missy."

"Just call her."

"She doesn't have her cell turned on. Says it breaks her concentration." Sara waved at Hayden as she headed down into the parking garage, muttering about revenge plots and the downfall of the Stratford Oaks.

Sara decided she wouldn't think about the Stratford Oaks; she would think about eating ice cream and soaking her feet.

She could have done without this extra hike because she had some spectacular blisters. What was with that? Stupid shoes. She tried adjusting her gait and putting weight on different parts of her feet until she reached the heavy brass-and-glass doors of the bar entrance. She pulled open the door and welcomed the whoosh of air conditioning.

She did not welcome the unsmiling man blocking her way. He wore a liverylike uniform meant to evoke old English gentry or guards or some such thing. The point was, he wasn't moving.

"Excuse me." She tried to walk around him.

"I'm sorry, miss. You can't come in here."

"It's okay. I need to tell my friend—"

"You don't have any friends in here."

"Yes, I do, she's—" Sara broke off. "I don't believe this." Had word gone out? Were she and Hayden on some call-girl watch list like the one for hot check writers?

She held up her foot. "Don't you see my shoes?"

"Yes, ma'am. They were one of the first things I noticed."

Quality, right. Three hundred bucks down the drain. "Look. I'm not a…a—"

"Sara?"

That voice. She knew that voice. Slowly, Sara turned and looked into the yummy chocolatey eyes of Simon Northrup.

5

SIMON HAD STARTED THINKING about women again. Not that he hadn't been thinking about women before, but the women who had been on his mind recently were Kayla—more of a woman-in-training—and her mother, Joanna, so he hadn't been thinking of women in the usual way. The, well, carnal way.

Of course, he'd once been madly, passionately in love with Joanna, and her betrayal had hurt. He'd moved on, although he'd be lying if he didn't admit noticing that Joanna still tried to push a button or two when it suited her purposes. Tall, haughty blondes hiding a molten center were his type, and she knew it.

But now there was Sara. She wasn't tall and she wasn't blond and he didn't know about any molten cores, but she'd become his new type.

Simon felt as though he'd been hibernating through a long female-less winter and it was now spring. Things were stirring once more. He was noticing women again, noticing everything about them. Their clothes, their shape, their hair, their perfume, their shoes and the way they walked. Whether they looked like Sara or not.

The woman walking just ahead of him on the sidewalk outside the hotel, for example, reminded him a little of Sara—or Sara in an alternate universe. This female's glorious legs flashed in and out of the long slit in her skirt while her hips swayed as only a women wearing a tight skirt and high-heeled shoes could sway them. Not Sara's style, but enjoyable.

Instead of paying attention to the conversations of the men he'd gone to the builders' convention to meet up with, he murmured politely as he watched the woman turn into the doorway of the Stratford Oaks. His interest quickened.

He needed this account. He was hustling for this account. And yet, he was ready to ditch the men and the account and pursue the woman just because she reminded him of Sara.

She was talking to the doorman as Simon and his group arrived, and then he caught her voice.

"Sara?" Though it couldn't be.

But it was. The legs...the walk...

She turned around and his mouth went dry. "Hi, Simon."

Breasts. She had breasts. He'd known that, but somehow, he'd missed their magnificence when he'd been killing space aliens with her.

So that *had* been Sara's walk and those *were* her legs and her mouth and her eyes and her...hair. There was more of that than he remembered, too. The best thing about her hair was that it was clipped back on one side to reveal the side of her neck and one perfect shell of an ear, waiting to be nibbled. Waiting for him to touch the tiny pearl stud with his tongue—

"Do you know this woman, Mr. Northrup?" the doorman asked.

Apparently not. "Yes. Sara works at my company. What are you doing here?" He'd completely forgotten the men behind him.

Her eyes were wide. Huge and dark and smudgy, as though she'd awakened after a night in his bed. Lord, she was sexy. Talk about molten cores. He stared at her, mesmerized.

"I'm...researching. Helping research, actually. I was here with Hayden Jones, one of our marketing account supervisors," she tossed back at the doorman, "and Melissa Morgan who's working in travel. We book a lot of business clients at this hotel and...well, we've heard things that concerned us, and rightly so," again to the doorman. "We came to see the hotel for ourselves." She gave Simon a brilliant smile. A blinding smile. A smile that rendered him mute.

"Hayden had to leave and I seem to be having trouble getting back inside to tell Missy. It seems unescorted women aren't welcome at the Stratford Oaks."

"Consider yourself escorted now." Simon took her arm, grateful for the excuse to touch her.

The doorman's face went professionally blank. "Ma'am, there seems to have been a misunderstanding."

She clutched Simon's arm. It felt good. He leaned against her.

"Oh, I understand," she was saying. "I understand that we'll recommend our female clients be booked elsewhere."

"I say, it's a bit warm out here," said one of the men on the sidewalk behind Simon.

Jolted out of his lustful Sara haze, Simon introduced her to them, finishing with, "And this is the sort of attention to detail you can expect from Avalli Digital."

"Well, I must say that I'm very impressed with the details." The man who had spoken leered at Sara.

She shrank back.

Simon caught his eye and drilled him with a look that made it clear that the woman next to him was no-leer territory.

They walked inside and Simon noticed that the doorman was conferring with the bartender and both were looking his way. "There's a story here, I'm thinking," he murmured to Sara.

She followed his gaze. "And I'm thinking I don't want to tell it to you."

He let it drop for now. "Have a drink with us?"

She was looking around. "I do need to talk to Missy...but I don't see her. Thanks for the offer, but I know you're busy."

"Stay." He didn't let go of her arm. The other men had staked out a table in the crowded room, waiting while the glasses and napkins left by the previous occupants were cleared away.

"I—"

"Please." His voice was low with a husky catch at

the end. Or maybe that was desperation. All he knew was that he needed to be with her just now. He couldn't remember the last time he'd felt this way.

She was so…something. Simon found himself wildly attracted to her in this incarnation. She was hot. Totally hot. Look-at-me hot. And Simon looked. He couldn't stop looking. He needed to pay attention to the men. He'd persistently courted them and the negotiations had reached a delicate stage at which the slightest thing could make them go either way. He'd already lost two accounts this week. Losing this one after all the time the account team had invested in the pitch would not be good for the bottom line.

And all he could think about was that directly above them were floors filled with many, many beds. He only needed one.

THAT WAS A GLEAM in Simon's eyes if ever she saw one. It was a hot gleam and it made Sara shiver. Against her better judgment, she heard herself order a Scotch rocks and then she sank onto a leather chair. Simon and his hot gleam sat in the chair next to hers. Oh, boy. No. Oh, man. She had captured all his manly attention. And he was a lot more man than she usually attracted, that was for sure. For the first time, she understood the term "man's man."

"So, lass, would you be workin' on our account?"

Sara dragged her eyes away from Simon. Who were these—right. They were with Simon. He'd introduced her, but she hadn't paid attention. She hoped there wasn't going to be a quiz.

Account... She glanced at Simon and saw him carefully watching the men, then glance her way. Would her working on the account be a good thing? A white-jacketed waiter wearing gloves set their drinks on the table.

Sara hefted hers and answered the man. "In a manner of speaking."

"A Scotch drinker. What a woman." The other men raised their glasses to her and everybody took a drink.

But not everybody wanted to spit it right back out the way Sara did. She forced herself to swallow and endure the burn all the way down. Vile, vile, vile. She munched on a few cheese crackers, but her tongue was numb and she couldn't taste anything.

Scotch, a martini or gin and tonic. She was going to get Missy for this—assuming she could find her and that Missy was still speaking to her when she did.

Speaking of speaking, nobody was saying anything. They were all looking at her. "So, have y'all ever been to Houston before?"

Two of the men had, but it was the first visit for one.

"I thought I was going to be dodging horses," he said. "Nobody told me it was the bloody tropics!"

Sara laughed politely and shot a quick look toward Simon. He gestured with his eyes toward the men, which Sara interpreted to mean that she was to stay and chat.

Cool. She'd never been the female entertainment before. But uncool being mistaken for a hooker. And she was pretty sure that most of the men at the Stratford Oaks, with the exception of Simon, were still laboring under the impression that she was a lady of the evening. Nevertheless, she channeled some Missy with a dash of Hayden and acquitted herself well, if she did say so herself.

But when they rose to go to dinner, she declined to go with them. "I know you boys have business to discuss." Oops. Too much Hayden.

Simon looked at his watch. "I'll give you a chance to unload the conference materials and meet you in the lobby in, say, ten minutes?"

One of the men leaned toward him. "Do ya think that's enough time to persuade yon lass to come with us?"

"Yon lass has other plans," Sara said, smiling her best Missy smile as she said it.

After the men left, Simon walked her past the bartender—with whom she exchanged a significant look—and opened the door for her.

"Thanks, Sara."

"For what?" She should be thanking him.

"You charmed those men. Thanks to you, I have every expectation of coming to an informal agreement with them over dinner tonight." The words were businesslike, but the way he said them was a warm caress. He took a step toward her.

In all honesty, she could have taken a step backward, and probably should have, but she didn't. He was looking down at her in such a lovely, manly, entirely inappropriate, gleaming way.

"I appreciate it," he said, still looking down at her, still standing a bit too close.

"You're welcome," she whispered. Oh, okay, she might have leaned a little toward him. Just in case he, you know, might be thinking of, well, kissing her.

Kissing Simon. Her hormones had quit prickling and had gone into complete meltdown. She could feel them pooling deep within her, sending little messages to her brain. "You're a woman. He's a man. We're ready. We're ready *now*. We've *been* ready."

Was she nuts? This couldn't be for real. She and Simon worked, if not exactly together, for the same company. A major no-no. He probably thought she expected a goodbye kiss and was just being nice so she wouldn't feel embarrassed.

But...there was that wonderful intense gleam in his eyes, and the way he focused on her and only her, compelling her to focus on him and only him. If she could just know what it was like to feel his mouth against hers, to be wrapped in his arms and pressed against his chest...

His head moved, tilting ever so slightly.

Desire crackled between them.

"Sara," he breathed.

She didn't even see his lips move. She closed her eyes as his hand skimmed around her cheek and cupped the back of her neck. She may have made a slight sound. She certainly tilted her chin.

His lips settled gently over hers in a questing, exploratory kiss. Sara knew he was judging her reaction, trying to figure out if they were both on the same page and what she wanted to do about it if they were. It was the perfect first kiss, especially considering they were in the outer entrance of a hotel bar in which she'd recently been mistaken for a hooker. It was the kind of first kiss that made her forget that Simon wasn't on her list of possibles.

As Simon broke the kiss, his hand slowly fell away and the look he gave her made her feel as though the U.S. Olympic gymnastics team was practicing in her stomach.

Oh, would it really be so bad to just forget about that little quibble she had with him? The one about his sis—

The unmistakable sound of a ringing cell phone echoed loudly in the glass vestibule. Both Sara and Simon checked their phones. It was his.

He pressed the talk button. "Kayla?"

Sara exhaled quietly. Simon shook his head at her to stay, then broke eye contact to concentrate on what his sister was saying. "But I told you I had a dinner meeting tonight. You should have checked with your mother. You'll just have to..."

Okay, it was a not-so-little quibble and a very timely reminder. She should leave. After all, Simon had already left her. Sara slipped out the door wondering if it was a good thing or a bad thing that Kayla had interrupted them.

"WHAT ARE YOU WEARING?" Hayden stared at her.

Not this again. "We're at a gym. I'm wearing gym clothes." Sara gestured to her baggy T-shirt and stretch shorts.

After the bar fiasco, Missy had offered to take them to the ritzy gym where her fiancé, Peter, worked out. Apparently, stressed out lawyers liked to work out there and lawyers, stressed out or not, fit Sara's ideal man profile. Sara wondered if they were capable of the complete devotion she required, but Missy had responded to her query with a huffy little, "Peter is *completely* devoted to me" and Sara figured it wasn't worth arguing the point.

"I've got your guest passes..." Missy trailed off when she saw Sara. "What's she wearing?" she asked Hayden.

"Workout clothes! Aren't we working out?" Sara gestured to the machines.

Missy, dressed in a too-cute pink and white tennis outfit, shook her head. "No. You'll, like, sweat."

"Well, yeah."

"That might not be a bad thing." Hayden wore black thigh-length, skin-tight shorts with a sports bra top accented with neon pink and orange. She was in full makeup. She even had on earrings. "Some men like a sweaty woman," she purred, already distracted by the view in the free-weight room.

"You know you have no intention of sweating," Missy said.

"Not on the machines, anyway."

"But, Missy, why the tennis outfit?" Sara asked.

Missy gave her a patient look. "So I can hang around the juice bar and look like I'm waiting for my court. The racquetball guys hang out there, too." She gave a little faraway smile. "Racquetball develops some interesting muscles."

"Does Peter know you're trolling for men?" Hayden asked.

"I was demonstrating how to, er, troll for Sara."

"Right."

They both looked at Sara and shook their heads.

"Okay, okay." She got the message already. "I'll go home and change."

"And put some makeup on," Hayden told her.

"Give your cheeks an extra swipe of blush so you'll look healthy," Missy added.

"Or I could just work out and blush for real!"

The problem was that Sara didn't have anything much to change into. Once at home, she put on some makeup and a slightly tighter T-shirt, then headed back to the gym.

The crowd had thickened.

Sara walked past the line waiting to sign in, and was intercepted by a black-spandex clad set of impressive muscles. "Did you sign in?"

"Uh, I'm a guest."

The man extended a giant paw. "May I see your pass?"

She remembered Missy holding out the passes, but

she didn't remember taking one. "My friend still has it. I was here earlier, but I didn't get the pass from her."

He wasn't buying her story. So what was this? Had Sara lost all credibility with men? "Where's your friend?" he asked.

Sara scanned the area for a pink and white tennis outfit. "She's probably at the bar where the tennis players hang out."

"Uh-huh. What's her name?"

Sara told him and he looked up Missy in the computer. "She's brought in her two-guest limit today."

"Yes, I'm one of those guests. Sara Lipton."

"Okay, I see you in the file."

"Good. Then I can go in?"

He shook his head. "You've already been in. One free visit per customer."

"But I never got—okay, can I just pay for today, then?"

"We don't do day passes."

What was she supposed to do now? She tried to find Hayden, but didn't see her, either.

"I can sign you up for a three-month trial membership."

"And how much is that?" Hadn't she been thinking about working out? This place would do as well as any other.

"There's a one-time thousand dollar registration fee—"

Sara's mind went numb at that point. Strike two in the Sara's-hunt-for-a-man campaign. She turned to leave and bumped into a solid wall of male flesh. "Sorry!" She stepped back and bounced off another set of pecs. "Oh, gosh, I'm so sorry—"

"Well, hello."

The pecs belonged to Simon Northrup. Simon Northrup in shorts and a T-shirt with the sleeves ripped off. Simon Northrup with his muscles exposed.

Oh, wow. The memory of their all-too-brief kiss burned on her lips.

He shifted his gym bag onto his shoulder. "Are you coming or going?"

"Going, I guess. I was only here on a guest pass and had to go back home for...something. There's no reentry. I never really got in at all."

"Well, come on." He dropped a hand onto her shoulder and steered her to the member sign-in area. "You can be my guest."

Every time she wrote him off, he managed to show up in time to rescue her. Once more, Simon was getting her into some place that didn't want her in. Sara started to tell him about the one-free-visit rule, but was distracted by the weight of his hand and his smooth take-charge attitude. Then there was their reflection in all those mirrors. Hunky muscle-y man and his woman. Okay, she was *glad* she'd changed into a tighter T-shirt, but there was nothing that could accessorize a girl like a good-looking male.

Simon whipped out a membership card and swiped it in the card reader, then tapped in something. A box next to the computer spit out a strip of paper. "Here you go." He handed it to her.

She waved it at the man who had challenged her earlier and walked right in. Now what? Simon had gone in through the men's locker room and Sara still didn't see Hayden anywhere. How was she supposed to approach men? They were all busy stretching and lifting and, er, sweating. Maybe she should hunt for Missy.

"Where are you headed first—the treadmill to warm up?" Simon appeared beside her, hands on hips. She'd thought he was going to go off and do his own thing.

"Um…" Sara looked in the treadmill direction and saw about two dozen machines lined up and an equal number of people dedicatedly walking and jogging to nowhere. "I guess so."

He chuckled. "Have you been here before?"

"No."

Simon's lips curved ever so slightly. "Have you ever been to a gym before?"

If you want a guy who's in shape, then he'll have to work out somewhere and he's going to want a girlfriend who works out, too. That had been Missy's advice yesterday and now Sara was facing Simon today, hesitant to admit that exercise had never been her thing. "I haven't been to a gym like this in a long time."

He gave her a quick once-over. "Then you must jog or something."

Bless his heart. "Or something."

"Shall I show you the machines?"

Simon stood before her in all his manliness. How

was she supposed to forget about him and go looking
for other men? Sara caved. "Oh, yes, please."

He started her off on a glider since the treadmills
were full.

It was kind of fun—like walking on air.

It was kind of fun for about three minutes, then Sara
began breathing a little harder and trying to hide it
from Simon, who was on the glider next to hers.

"I looked for you yesterday at work," he said, not
sounding breathy at all.

"Oh?" she managed.

"We got the Tripplehorn account out of Glasgow."

"Great!" One-word responses. That was the ticket.
That and breathing deeply and maybe not taking such
very large steps and just hanging on rather than working the arm thingies.

"Thanks again for your help. They were impressed
that our company was personally surveying the hotel.
And so am I."

"Hmm." She was going to have to alert Missy and
Hayden so they could get their stories straight. Missy
had been in the restroom, and when she'd come out
and hadn't seen Sara or Hayden, she'd left, too. Sara
had hoped she wouldn't have to tell the others that
she'd gone back inside.

"You'll want to pace yourself when you're just starting out," he said and Sara realized she'd been huffing
and puffing.

He was going to think she was out of shape. Well,
she was, but weren't men rebelling against hard and

skinny female bodies? She'd read an article to that effect and it had certainly made sense, so Sara had deliberately gone for the soft, pillowy form.

Maybe her pillow had become a little too lumpy.

She slowed down, then got off the machine and tried to stand on jelly legs. "I think I'm warmed up now."

Simon checked the timer on her machine. Not even ten minutes. How embarrassing. Still, without a word, he got off the glider and beckoned her to the room filled with black and white machines that did who-knew-what forms of torture. Sara figured she was about to find out.

"Let's start you off with some biceps curls."

Oh, good. Her legs could rest. And her biceps ought to be pretty developed since she was forever carrying heavy boxes of employee records all over the place.

With Simon directing her, Sara straddled a bench, lay her arms down an inclined pad and positioned her wrists beneath two padded rolls. Simon was busying himself adjusting the weights.

"Okay, one at a time, slowly bring your arms toward you."

"Okay." She pulled and nothing happened. "It's stuck."

"Stand up."

Simon took her place and placed his arms in position. He brought the padded roll back so hard, Sara thought he was going to break the machine. Talk about biceps.

Yes, talk about biceps and triceps and all the other ceps that were so nicely on display.

His mouth quivered at the corner. "It seems to be unstuck now."

"Yes, thanks." Sara hesitated, then against her better judgment, she extended her index finger. "Is, um, that," she drew her finger down the bulge in his arm, "the biceps?"

Danger, danger, danger. He looked down at her finger, and his head bent until their foreheads were nearly touching.

"Yes."

"It's so...big. And hard." She traced the outline of the muscle. "You must work out a lot."

"Two or three times a week keeps me in shape."

"I could manage two or three times a week."

A couple of beats of silence went by. "You would be amazed at how great you'd feel."

"Would I?"

He gazed intently into her eyes. "Yes."

And Sara didn't know if they were still talking about muscles and working out, or something else.

She withdrew her hand and reluctantly straddled the machine again. Positioning her arms, she pulled. Fire erupted up and down her arms.

"Hang on." Simon humiliatingly removed half the weights. "You shouldn't try too much too soon."

This time, the machine cooperated and Sara managed ten reps, which was the number recommended to beginners. Still, her muscles trembled and she didn't think it was because Simon stood watching her, his lips curved in amusement. "Atta girl. Come over here." He moved to the next machine and began removing weights.

"We'll work your legs now to give your arms time to recover."

Sara could use the recovery time.

"Hop on the bench face-down. This machine does virtually the same thing, but for the muscles in the back of your legs—your hamstrings."

Oh, this was not good. Sara did not want to lie face-down with her, er, gluteus very maximus on view. Especially since Simon's was so tight and, well, un-maximal.

Trying to hide her reluctance, Sara gripped the hand bars and positioned herself on the narrow bench. She did not feel at her most attractive.

"Draw your heels toward your—"

"Okay." She pulled and whoa, there was another set of muscles screaming at her.

"Too much?"

"Yes." Pride wasn't an issue anymore. Pain was.

"I'm surprised. Your legs look to be in great shape."

Mollified, Sara didn't notice that he'd failed to remove any weights until she conked out after seven reps. "Uh..." She felt like a beached whale. "If you could just..." Blindly, she waved one of her hands around until Simon grabbed onto her. Holding wasn't enough. He had to tug her up as well.

Only she didn't seem to be moving.

Along with new muscle groups, Sara was learning about new depths of humiliation. Determined now to stand and wipe the concerned expression off Simon's face, she fairly leaped to her feet and felt her thigh contract painfully. "Ow!" She limped frantically.

"Cramp?"

"Yes, it's a cramp!" she snapped.

"Which leg?" Simon maneuvered her to the floor right in front of everyone, though Sara wasn't in a position to care.

"Both legs!"

"Keep them bent about ninety degrees while I bring them toward your head. Hold onto your calves."

His warm hands pressed against her thigh muscles as he flexed and released her legs. She wished she could enjoy it.

Sara looked at Simon moving back and forth above her as he flexed her legs. Fate had given her what she'd lusted for, with an amusing little twist.

"Having fun, you two?" Hayden's face appeared upside down in Sara's field of vision. The day just kept getting better and better.

"Sara has leg cramps."

"How resourceful of you, Sara."

"Hayden," she warned.

"Why am I not surprised that you're a member here, Simon?"

"I have no idea, Hayden."

Sara saw only the underside of their chins as they faced each other over her. Simon had the tiniest curved scar just beneath his that Sara would never have seen otherwise. It was as though she'd discovered one of his little secrets.

"Why, it's because you're in such good shape."

Hayden was flirting with Simon. Flirting right over Sara's nearly dead body. Typical Hayden.

"Thanks."

Hmm. Simon wasn't flirting back. He was, however, massaging her thighs. Right in front of Hayden. Hmm. Could be good.

The cramp was going. Now if Hayden would only go, too, Sara could begin to enjoy herself. She wondered how long she could fake a cramp.

"Sara, hon, are you feeling any better?" Hayden's bright eyes were directed at her.

"Yes. Lots better."

"I'll just bet you are. When you're back on your feet, come find me. I ran into somebody I want you to meet."

Gee, thanks a lot, Hayden.

That wasn't fair. Sure, Hayden liked to cause trouble, but Sara had declared herself uninterested in Simon.

What a joke. She was incredibly interested in Simon and right now, it looked as though he was incredibly interested in her.

She had to put a stop to it. "I think I'm fine now. I'd like to try standing."

He leaned back on his heels and she sat up. The

movement brought her a lot closer to Simon than she'd expected.

He didn't move away. "Sara..."

Ignoring everyone around them, he drew one warm hand along her arm, over her shoulder, then grasped her nape.

Was he going to kiss her again? Here? Now?

Was she going to let him? Here? Now?

"Simon..." Wrong time, wrong place and, most unfortunately, wrong man.

He rubbed his thumb against her neck. "Have lunch with me?"

"I have other plans," she said firmly.

His eyes roamed her face. "Dinner, then."

"Uh..." Be strong. "Uh" was not strong.

"Or my favorite meal with a woman, breakfast."

She caught her breath. Breakfast would come after... She swallowed. "I—I don't eat breakfast." Weak. And untrue.

His mouth creased in a lazy half smile. "Then start. I make a mean omelet."

Simon cooking for her. Simon cooking for her while wearing boxers or sweatpants...barefoot...shirtless... sexy shaving stubble...his hair a little curly because he hadn't tamed it for the day.

"Simon, I don't think it would be a good idea." Because it was a most excellent idea.

His fingers stopped their mesmerizing movement.

"How long are you going to ignore this thing between us?"

Sara struggled out from beneath his arm and got to her feet. She was a little shaky, but capable of walking. Around them, machines clanked and people strained and sweated. It was not the place for a conversation like this, but it was long past time. "I'm ignoring it until I know I won't get hurt. I want a relationship, not to scratch an itch."

"Sara!" He got to his feet with an athlete's grace. "How could you think—"

"Now, look. You've got a job where you work long, crazy hours and you have a kid sister who needs you. You don't want a relationship. All you've got is an itch."

His eyes darkened. "Nice speech. But there's one problem."

"What?"

"You don't know what the hell you're talking about." His biceps curled around her and drew her hard against his pecs—his hard pecs. She, in contrast, was all quivering flesh.

He kissed her just as hard, demonstrating that his mouth was in as good shape as the rest of him.

Sara went boneless. When he abruptly set her from him, he had to steady her on her feet as she embarrassingly lurched toward him.

"Well?"

Was there steam coming off her? She cleared her throat and tucked a stray lock of hair behind her ear.

"I—the way you kiss isn't the problem. Your technique is fine. Really," she added when he raised an eyebrow. "Actually...more than fine."

He gave her a purely male smile. "Glad to hear it."

"But you still have other priorities in your life."

"I can't think of any right now." He took a step toward her.

"I can." Sara backed away. "And I don't want to compete. So...I'll just say thanks and—" she continued putting space between them "—goodbye."

6

"HONEY, IF YOU DON'T scratch that itch, somebody else will."

"I don't want to talk about it." Sara shoved a forkful of creamy potato salad into her mouth. She also had a scoop of creamy chicken salad on her tray as well as a slice of coconut cream pie. Comfort cream.

"I cannot get over the fact that you were lying on your back with your legs spread *wide* open in front of God and everybody and Simon Northrup was...was..." Missy was so scandalized she couldn't even get the words out.

"Massaging her thighs," Hayden supplied with a snicker.

"Her upper thighs!" Missy ended in a squeak. "A hundred years ago and you two would have been engaged by now."

"Thanks a lot." Sara shoved in another mouthful. Chicken salad this time. Going straight to those very same thighs, no doubt.

Missy tapped her pen—the silver one engraved with the date she became engaged. "I don't think having Sara meet men directly is working."

Hayden snorted. "It's working just fine, I'd say!"

"Just shut up," Sara mumbled and went for the coconut cream pie. She hadn't told them about the kiss and she wasn't going to.

"Sara..." Missy covered her hand—the one that wasn't shoveling coconut cream into her mouth. "Are you sure you don't want to reconsider Simon?"

Sara ruthlessly repressed the memories of his hands on her thighs, the muscles in his arms and the wave of hair that fell over his forehead in a way he wouldn't have allowed it to at the office. Most especially, she suppressed the memory of being crushed against his chest with his hot lips on hers. That was a really hard one to suppress. "I have been down that road before."

"But never in a Rolls, honey," Hayden said. "And Simon is definitely a Rolls."

"It doesn't matter what kind of car it is, when it runs out of gas, it isn't going to go. I'm looking for a guy who's willing to carry gas cans."

"But why, when there are gas stations on every corner?" Missy asked.

"It's a metaphor, Missy." Sara finished her pie. "Forget about Simon." She hoped she could.

"Okay, if Simon isn't for you, then he's not. But, Sara, is it really that hopeless?"

Sara visualized Kayla and Joanna. Visualized Simon's instant response to interruptions. Visualized the number of interruptions. Visualized herself whining about the interruptions. Visualized what might be getting interrupted. "Yes!"

"Okay, okay." Missy presented her with yet another

spreadsheet. "The fine arts and couples who met through them cross-referenced with occupation and income of the male."

Hayden pulled the spreadsheet toward her before Sara could see it. "Where do you get this information?"

"If you'd been in a sorority, you wouldn't have to ask. Now, Sara, do you happen to have an affinity for the arts?"

"I had an affinity for an Art once. Art Rosenbloom. He didn't say much." Hayden smiled. "But he didn't have to."

Sara ignored her. "I played clarinet in seventh grade, was in chorus in eighth grade, and in high school my ecology poster won third place in a district-wide contest. That was so cool. It was a collage thing and I had live worms in this cute little cage that I'd spray-painted gold and attached to the poster. I was showing how composting can enrich..." She trailed off as she became aware of Hayden and Missy wearing identical "ick" expressions. "And I've seen the *Nutcracker* twice," she finished.

There was silence as everybody stared at the spreadsheet.

"The average ballet volunteer is nearly a decade younger than that of the other volunteers," Missy offered. "A lot of mothers get involved when their little girls start dance lessons."

"And this will help Sara how?" Hayden stole a forkful of Sara's leftover chicken salad.

"She can make contact with women her own age

who probably know eligible single men. Plus their mothers who may have unmarried sons."

Hayden gazed at her consideringly. "Could work."

"Well, she *has* seen the *Nutcracker* twice." Missy cleared her throat and smiled a determinedly perky smile at Sara. "Ballet it is, then."

SIMON HAD SPENT way too much time reliving the incident at the gym, specifically those moments when he'd finally got his hands on Sara. He'd used an undoubtedly painful cramp of a major muscle group as an excuse to touch her. How desperate was that? Not as desperate as kissing her was. He closed his eyes as he relived the fire that had burned from his mouth to his groin as he'd kissed her. He hadn't cared about time or place or circumstances.

No wonder she'd fled and he hadn't seen her since. What had he expected when he'd hit on her with all the finesse of a hormone-saturated teenager?

Speaking of teenagers, Joanna had called him in a panic because some thirteen-year-old boy had been calling Kayla and what should she do?

Simon told her that talking on the phone seemed fairly innocuous, but apparently it was more than talking on the phone, it was instant-messaging and setting up personal Web pages that dripped with sexual references.

Great. Instead of figuring out how to approach Sara, he'd spent last night cruising preteen Web pages and feeling very old and out of touch in the process. He considered himself media savvy, but those pages had managed to shock him.

Were the kids serious? Or were they just parroting the sexual references in advertising and pop culture without really understanding them?

Somehow, he found himself taking Kayla out for a hamburger and trying to talk to her about it. Kayla became as sullen as ever, Joanna was contemptuous of his efforts and he'd let three days go by without contacting Sara.

Temporarily backing off a relationship with her was probably wise, he told himself. Now, he'd start again slowly with a Sunday jazz brunch at Brennan's. Sunday noon was nice and respectable; there were no hidden pressures about nighttime sleeping arrangements. No external ones, anyway.

He'd make reservations and call her right now.

Simon was on the phone with Brennan's when another call came through.

"Northrup," he answered.

"Simon, it's Joanna. Listen, there's something wrong with the computer and Kayla has a project due tomorrow...."

WHEN SHE'D IMAGINED her adult life, Sara had never envisioned herself wearing a silk shirtwaist dress with a matching fabric belt—how frumpy was that?—expensive and uncomfortable black pumps and a string of good-quality fake pearls as she called people on a list and asked them for large amounts of money.

It was surreal. It was also excruciating because Sara had had no experience asking people for money—her parents excepted. And even then, she was expected to wash the car or do the dishes for a week in return. Somehow offering to wash someone's car after she thanked them "for your generous support in the past" and would they "consider becoming a Green Room Patron," which was ten thousand dollars, didn't seem quite enough.

These people were complete and total strangers, and yet, here she was, cheerily asking them to part with thousands of dollars. And an astounding percentage did so. Who knew?

Sara had been given several sneaky phone scripts, which meant that she'd never look at charity calls the same way again.

"Mrs. Norris? Sara Lipton here with the Barre Belles. We're just finalizing our guest list for the pre-season dinner honoring the ballet patrons. May we include you this year?"

"Sara Lipton," mused a cigarette-roughened voice. "You're new, aren't you?"

"Yes, ma'am."

"Lipton...Lipton... Do I know your mother?"

"I don't believe so."

"Hmph. So is Patty Wickham on the Green Room list this year?"

"Just a minute." Sara set down the phone, walked over to the computer and brought up the file with the donor list. Fortunately for the ballet, it appeared that the Green Room was going to be crowded this year.

"Yes, she is," she told Mrs. Norris when she got back to her phone.

"Thank you, young lady." She sounded elated, which probably meant Sara wasn't supposed to give out that information. Too late. "Sign me up for the Director's Circle."

Twenty-five thousand dollars. Just like that. And the woman didn't even know her. "I—thank you, Mrs. Norris. I mean, the Barre Belles appreciate your support of the fine arts in Houston. Being a member of the Director's Circle entitles—"

"I know what it entitles me to. Now you listen here. If Patty Wickham upgrades, I'm counting on you to let me know. You're Sara Lipton. I've written down your name."

"Yes, ma'am."

Sara hung up the phone thinking that if she were as ruthless as the rest of them, she'd give Patty Wickham a heads-up, then call Mrs. Norris. Instead, she checked the woman's name off her list.

Actually, it wasn't so bad being a member of the Barre Belles. Missy had got her in through a sorority sister and Sara already had three offers to introduce her to unmarried male relatives. Not bad for a Saturday morning.

Sara held up her sheet of paper. "Barbara, I'm finished."

Barbara had been a Barre Belle for years and years.

Enough years to have a grandson she wanted Sara to meet. Barbara was cool, so Sara was hopeful that some of the coolness had filtered down through the generations.

"Where did your list leave off?"

"With the *n*'s. Mrs. Norris. She's a new member of the Director's Circle," Sara couldn't help mentioning.

"Well done, Sara! Did you ring the bell?"

"Bell?"

"When you sign up a Director's Circle, you get to ring the bell." Barbara handed her a brass bell with tiny ballet slippers on the handle. "Go ahead. Ring it."

Hayden would laugh at her. Missy would be thrilled for her. Sara rang the bell and there were exclamations and applause from the other women manning the phone banks.

"Denise Norris," Barbara called out.

Sara accepted everyone's congratulations, then Barbara handed her another computer printout. "You're doing so well, here are the rest of the *n*'s."

Well, she was on a roll, wasn't she? Sara reached for the phone and then saw the first name on her list: Simon Northrup.

No. Simon and the ballet? Yeah, right. Houston was a big city; there was bound to be more than one Simon Northrup.

But that first phone number looked awfully familiar. The Avalli digital main line. It figured. Kayla was probably into ballet and that mother of hers had taken advantage of Simon. That didn't mean that Sara would. There was no way she was calling Simon Northrup to ask him for money. Not after...she shivered at the thought of it.

It was Saturday, so he wouldn't be at work, at least officially. No point in calling him. Except that his home number was also there in bold, which meant it was an unlisted number.

Well, she wasn't calling it, and that was final. Simon Northrup was not donating to the ballet this year, unless he remembered all on his own.

When she turned in her list, Barbara glanced through it. "Simon Northrup didn't contribute?"

"He's still considering," Sara said.

And she didn't feel the slightest bit guilty.

"SIMON NORTHRUP, why are you giving that sweet Sara such a hard time?"

Simon was nonplused. How could Barbara Franks of the Barre Belles know about Sara?

Simon liked to stand and stretch when he took phone calls at his desk, but this one had him rooted to the spot. "Sara?" he prompted carefully.

"Sara Lipton, one of our new girls. She has such a knack for fund-raising that I'm surprised you didn't fall under her spell."

Oh, he'd fallen, all right, but the spell caster was avoiding him. She hadn't returned his call, the one in which he'd planned to invite her to brunch, so he was thinking of paying a casual visit to the twenty-fourth floor, though it could be tricky spending too much time with her at work. Interoffice dating wasn't frowned upon, but there was an unwritten rule against it.

However, it *was* unwritten and Simon was practically a department all by himself. He rarely interacted with domestic employees, since his work was overseas. And he never visited the payroll department.

By the time Barbara Franks got ahold of him, Simon had thought up an impressive list of reasons why dating a fellow employee was not only okay, but desirable. Now if he could only find a casual way to approach Sara.

"Don't tease her, Simon."

So Sara was volunteering with the Barre Belles, Simon mused. Interesting. And possibly useful. "What makes you think I'm teasing her?"

"By telling her you're still considering making a donation!" She laughed. "You men. Don't think I don't know that you only want to talk to her again. But just a word—she's new at this and might think you're serious."

Good. Great. In fact, an excuse to approach Sara had just dropped in his lap. An expensive excuse, but he'd take it.

SARA WAS extremely proud of herself. She was only thinking about Simon once every hour or so, down from every five minutes, which had been a huge improvement over thinking about him constantly.

She had also declined to run up to the twenty-sixth floor when Hayden called with a potential paper jam.

She even cut off Hayden at lunch when she reported on the stupid jam and how Simon had fixed it.

She hadn't even strayed from her course when Missy reported her findings on Barbara Franks's grandson—two years younger than Sara and an unemployed history major, therefore Not Eligible.

But honestly, how was she supposed to stop thinking about him when he softly knocked on her cubicle wall and smiled down at her, making her remember that the last time he'd looked down at her he was massaging her thighs?

"Hi, Sara."

Omigosh, that voice. Just his voice could turn her into a puddle. She didn't even need to think about the way his arms had looked in the ripped T-shirt or the way his strong, warm hands had felt kneading and rubbing and caressing...

"Hi!" Too bright, too peppy.

"I hear you're interested in the ballet?"

Oh, God. He'd heard...he'd heard what? "Well, you know, uh, the *Nutcracker*..."

He gave her an amused look. "Yes. I know it well."

Couldn't she appear competent around him at least once? Was that really too much to ask?

"I understand it's time for the Barre Belles' annual appeal."

"Yes, the donors' dinner and all that." She stared at her desk.

"I've considered my donation for this year..."

He knew. He knew because Barbara Franks had called him behind her back. Sara cringed.

A check appeared in her field of vision. He slid it smoothly across her desk. "I thought I'd save you the trouble of a phone call."

Green Room level. Sara's head shot up.

Simon's lips curved in that way he had, as though he was on the verge of smiling. And his eyes...well, she wouldn't even go there.

"Wow. I mean, the Barre Belles appreciate your support of the fine arts in Houston. A Green Room patron is entitled—"

He waved away the rest of her speech and leaned against her cubicle doorway. "I'm only interested in being able to take Kayla to the *Nutcracker* tea with the dancers."

Right. Kayla. Sara was trying to forget about Simon, but she'd challenge any woman to forget about a man who could drop a five-figure check just so his sister could meet some ballet dancers.

Yes, there was something wildly attractive about a man who could hand over a check that large without asking that she wait a few days before cashing it, or grousing about the new car part or electronic toy or the sports tickets he could have bought instead.

She should say something, something not written in the Barre Belles' fund-raising guidebook. "This is really generous of you. Kayla is lucky to have you for a big brother."

His smile dimmed slightly.

Sara hurried on. "Do you have to pick her up from school today, or anything? If not, how about a cup of coffee?"

"Sounds good." And now he did smile. "I could use a jolt of caffeine."

Omigosh. Sara hadn't expected him to agree.

There was a Starbucks in the underground tunnel system connecting the buildings downtown. She swallowed. "Starbucks okay?"

"Perfect."

Damn. "Can you go now?" she asked. "Maybe later would be better if you're busy—"

"Now is fine." He straightened.

Well, she had no choice, did she? The man had just handed her a huge check. It would have been churlish to take it and run.

They walked in silence to the elevator. Then it opened, and they were the only two people inside. Sara was alone with Simon Northrup and a couple of her most recent elevator fantasies: the ever popular getting-stuck-in-the-elevator fantasy, and the Simon-pushing-on-the-emergency-stop-so-he-could-kiss-her-senseless fantasy....

"Any ill effects from your workout on Saturday?"

That line of dialogue was not in either of her fantasies. "I'm fine."

"Good."

She took a step to the side, putting a little more distance between them. It was better if she couldn't feel the heat from his body because it reminded her of the way his hands had felt and, well, that wasn't good.

"Sara..."

She stared at the floor numbers. "Yes?" If he said anything to her about Saturday or itching or breakfast, or that short, searing kiss, she'd punch the emergency stop herself. In fact, she might punch it anyway. She no longer cared about what was best for her future. Carpe diem, and all that. At least, carpe Simon. She turned to him.

He stared down at her with that intense look that promised equally intense lovemaking. A shiver rippled through her.

She licked her lips. That always worked in the movies. Sure enough, Simon's gaze caught the movement. He opened his mouth and Sara held her breath.

"So how long have you been interested in the ballet?"

ALL HE WANTED to do was stop the elevator and kiss her senseless.

Okay. Calm. Think. Make conversation. Do not touch. Do not stop elevator and kiss Sara.

Simon knew he'd created this awkwardness between them by coming on too strong Saturday. He wouldn't make that mistake again because Sara was worth waiting for.

She volunteered for the ballet. He wouldn't have thought it of her, which meant there were more layers to explore and the more he found, the more he liked.

She'd been casually fun with Kayla, sexy as hell at the Stratford Oaks, bent on improving herself—adorably—at the gym, and now here she was determined to contribute to her community by working with the ballet.

She was a winner. As close to perfect as a woman could be. And if he wanted any kind of chance with this perfect woman, then he'd better proceed cautiously. So. He needed a nice neutral topic. She liked ballet, he'd start there.

"Saturday was my first day volunteering. I, well, when I was little, I liked the *Nutcracker*."

"Kayla tried out for the part of Clara a couple of years ago." And when she didn't get it, she'd thrown such a fit that his father had tried to buy her way in. He didn't succeed, for which Simon was thankful. He could only imagine how bad Kayla would be now if she'd learned that she could buy her way into and out of situations. She'd learn that soon enough. "She didn't get the part, but she enjoyed being in the party scene," was all Simon elected to tell Sara.

"That's nice." She stared fixedly at the floor indicator lights.

This wasn't going as smoothly as he would have hoped. "What's your favorite ballet?"

She gave him a quick look as the elevator doors opened. "The, uh, *Nutcracker*."

"Yes, it's a real crowd pleaser. When I was growing up in London, I saw Baryshnikov dance." Women liked Baryshnikov. Sara should respond to that.

"In the *Nutcracker?*"

Damn the *Nutcracker*. "No. In *Romeo and Juliet*."

"Oh."

They turned right as they exited the elevator and headed toward Starbucks.

Simon tried again. "It's always amazed me that a city with no basements has a complete underground tunnel system."

"They come in handy," Sara said.

They got in line. There was always a line at Starbucks.

"What would you like?" she asked.

"A latte."

"I'm having the caramel one. It's super sweet, but I didn't have dessert at lunch."

So polite. So stilted. He hated that he'd ruined their easy camaraderie. It was his own fault for pushing. He knew she was different, yet he'd treated her the same way he'd treated women with whom he'd only intended to have brief encounters.

He'd just have to try harder. "The men from Glasgow have faxed over a preliminary agreement. I know that you helped influence them."

She blushed. A woman who blushed in this day and age? Simon was charmed. "They asked about you," he added and watched her blush deepen.

"They don't think I'm part of the marketing team, do they?"

"You're on the Avalli Digital team, therefore, in a sense you are on the team."

"You know what I mean. You marketing guys can put a spin on anything."

They reached the barista and Sara ordered. She already had her wallet out, so he let her pay, too, because it seemed to be something she was determined to do. He liked that. It had been a long time since a woman had treated him.

He tried not to think about it, but even Joanna had never asked him over for a meal. Not that Joanna cooked. But take-out would have been okay—it was the thought that was important here.

"Do you cook?" he asked Sara suddenly, imagining her inviting him over for a home-cooked meal.

Startled, she looked at him. "I *can* cook—I think. But I rarely cook. I grill and microwave, if that counts."

"That counts."

"I don't really do fancy stuff for just myself. I take a veggie dish to my parents' for the holidays. That kind of thing."

At last an opening. "Where do your parents live?"

"They've retired to Wimberly."

"The Hill Country. It's a beautiful place."

Simon had been willing to sit and talk at a table, but to his disappointment, Sara began to walk back to the elevator once they got their coffees.

She didn't even look at him. He wanted to ask her to the jazz brunch, but figured she'd turn him down.

He had only a few minutes to try to break through her reserve. "Are you planning to work out at the club any time this week?"

"I'm not a member and," she gave a little laugh, "I can't afford that place."

"You...you could be my guest...."

The elevator doors opened. "I think they have rules against that."

Yes, they did, but Simon could have figured a way round it.

There were people inside the elevator and he didn't think he could continue the conversation without sounding desperate.

He got out with her on the twenty-fourth floor. "Thanks for the coffee." If she would just look at him...

And then she did and he wished she hadn't. "It was the least I could do for a Green Room donor." She smiled. He recognized it as the professional business woman's smile, coolly friendly without a hint of anything sexual or personal or encouraging.

"I hope you find a gym to join."

"I hope so, too." She smiled and nodded. "Thanks again." And she turned down the hallway.

It was a classic brush-off. Simon stared after her unable to figure out what he was doing wrong.

KEEP WALKING *keep walking keep walking.*

That was awful. Horrible. Simon probably thought she was a cultural vacuum with no conversation. She wasn't an expert by any means, but she had paid attention in art and music appreciation classes. It was just that she couldn't get past her overwhelming attraction to him and access her brain.

It didn't matter now. Simon was probably no more. Not that he ever was, except there was the matter of the gleam. Missy and Hayden had said she'd know it when she saw it and she'd definitely seen it—or was that a reflection of her own gleam? No, she hadn't imagined that kiss in the Stratford Oaks doorway or the hot little sampler at the gym. She hadn't imagined his invitation to multiple meals including breakfast.

But she'd completely rejected him. Twice now. Okay. Then this was what she was going to do: she'd attempt once more to meet another man and go the ring and veil route. And if that didn't work, then she'd try to reinstate that gleam in Simon's eye and go for a long smooth ride in a Rolls.

7

"You try to wear those pearls inside and I'll strangle you with them!"

Missy's hand crept to her neck. "Pearls are always appropriate—"

"Not at an Astros game, sweetie. This is my turf. You wear clothes that are bright and tight, show some skin, and cop an attitude." Hayden had started early on the attitude.

"I'd counted on the pearls to cancel out the fact that I'm going to have to drink beer from a plastic cup."

Maybe going to an Astros game wasn't such a good idea, Sara thought. But Hayden had been insistent, and had convinced Missy without too much trouble, that Sara's ideal man would like baseball. Something about testosterone calling to testosterone.

Since she'd gone with Missy's advice on the Barre Belles thing, Sara had acquiesced to Hayden's instructions to wear a tight top, preferably red, and preferably low cut enough to warrant rescuing the Wonderbra from the back corner of her underwear drawer. "You want to attract the attention of the camera guy," Hayden had advised them. "He'll put your picture up on the big screen and interested parties can check you out.

Truly interested parties will find you during the seventh inning stretch."

"Hayden, thousands of people will be at the game. I hardly think we're going to be singled out," Missy had replied.

That's kind of what Sara had thought, but Hayden was insistent. She'd also insisted that they go to an afternoon game which meant that they'd snuck out of work early—along with a surprisingly large proportion of the downtown working population. As Hayden and Missy argued over pearls, Sara watched youngish business types in button-down shirts and slacks stream past them into Minute Maid Park. Hayden was right. There could be nice hunting here.

"The pearls go in the purse, sugar." Hayden withheld Missy's ticket.

"All right!" Missy unclasped her necklace, wrapped the pearls in a tissue and tucked them carefully in her purse, which she then clutched tightly to her side.

Missy had on a high-necked sleeveless knit shell that she'd worn beneath her suit jacket. She'd left the jacket in the car.

"As a point of information, why haven't you complained about Missy wearing black?" Sara asked.

Hayden handed out the tickets. "It's tight and she's a blonde. 'Nuff said."

Missy fluffed her hair and took the ticket.

Sara pondered the unfair advantages blondes had over the rest of the population as they entered the stadium and searched for their seats.

"I can't believe I let you talk me into taking off early from work," Missy said. And actually, Sara was feeling a few guilt twinges as well.

Hayden wasn't. "We work hard. We deserve a break. And just think—men in tight white pants."

"But I'm paid by the hour."

Sara had forgotten that Missy worked for a temp agency. "I appreciate this, Missy."

"Oh, it's good for me to do something out of character. It'll keep Peter interested. And won't he be surprised when I can talk baseball with him? Do they print a glossary in the back of the programs or something?"

They were all walking toward the section with their seats when Hayden suddenly peeled off and stood in line at a concession stand.

"What is she—beer!" Missy gasped. "It's not even four-thirty yet."

It seemed kind of early for beer to Sara, too. But Hayden beckoned them over.

"Oh, it's not for me." She gave them a knowing smile. "It's for the camera guys."

"What camera guys?" Sara asked.

"For the big screen. We're paying them a little visit. How will they find me if they don't know where to look?"

Missy nodded her head and grinned at Sara. "She's good."

Sara couldn't believe it, but Hayden made them all carry a beer, go through the "Authorized Personnel

Only" door, and climb about a million stairs to one of the broadcast boxes, where she proceeded to flirt with the lighting techs and the guy who ran the big-screen camera. She left her ticket stub and the beers. Then and only then did they make their way to their seats.

"Inhale and keep your shoulders back, Sara. Oh, and when it's time for the 'Star-Spangled Banner,' we're going to just sing our little hearts out."

"I'm not real good with the high notes," Sara mumbled.

"Mouth the words, honey, and keep smiling."

"I can't tell you how impressed I am by your attention to detail, Hayden," Missy smiled as she spoke. Missy did smiling very well.

"You aren't the only one who schemes."

They'd been sitting for several minutes watching the warm-ups. Sara was getting a little light-headed from all the deep breathing she was doing. At least her mother would be proud of her posture.

"Change seats," Hayden ordered her abruptly. "We're both in red and we need Missy in the middle for contrast."

Missy was standing up as soon as Hayden mentioned the red part.

Honestly, Sara had so much to learn.

And then Missy screamed in her ear. "Wave, y'all!"

And there was Hayden—and then all of them on the big screen. Sara almost forgot to breathe. Hayden got to her feet and blew kisses to the players who were running to the dugout as warm-ups ended. The camera followed her and Missy and Sara were out of the shot.

"I have certainly underestimated her," Missy murmured in Sara's ear.

"If there's one thing I've learned, it's to never underestimate Hayden. Hey, Hayden—how did you learn about the camera guys?"

"I'm in charge of stadium ads for Avalli, remember?" She sat down and preened.

Several minutes later, an usher beckoned to Hayden. "Excuse me, ma'am?"

"And so it begins," she said. "This one is a real eager beaver. Yes?" she called down the row.

"You and your friends are invited to watch the game from one of the club suites."

Missy gripped Sara's arm. *"The club suites."*

"Whose club suite?" Hayden asked.

Now Missy gripped Hayden's arm. "Does it matter?"

"Why, yes." Hayden looked at her in surprise. "We might get a better offer."

"Does this happen to you a lot?" Sara asked.

"Only when I go to an Astros game."

It figured.

Hayden asked again, but the usher cupped his hand to his ear and shook his head.

She stood. "Come on, ladies. We can always leave."

"You know," Sara said as they followed the usher to the club level. "I wonder how I ever met any men at all without you two."

"You met men," Missy answered her. "You just didn't meet quality men."

"Oh." The usher had indicated which suite and Hayden stopped short, hands on hips. "I didn't know international marketing rated a suite. I'm thinking I'll have a chat with our finance officer."

"What are you talking about?" Sara asked.

Hayden stood aside and pointed through the glass. Sara saw Simon and a group of people that included the Glasgow men, Kayla, Amber and Joanna.

But mostly she saw Simon. Saw the quick, pleased smile as his gaze caught and held hers. Took in the casual knit shirt that subtly reminded her of the muscles beneath, the khaki slacks...the man did look good in slacks.

And those eyes. She saw the gleam, even from this distance, and saw it change into something more. A warm shiver rolled through her. Yeah, shivers were cold, but Sara's felt warm and were getting warmer by the second.

How could he do that to her with just a look across a crowded luxury sports box?

I'm a man. You're a woman. I'm interested. Your move.

Her move.

It looked like her move was going to be tossing the ring and veil and hitching a ride in a Rolls.

She could no longer resist him. How could she settle down with another man when Simon was, incredibly, available to her? Her future was just going to have to wait. *Eyes Wide Open*, she told herself. *Simon will put*

*work and his sister ahead of you. And Joanna will be right
there to see that you don't distract him. And he won't stop
her. And after he doesn't stop her one too many times, that
will be the end of it.*

Even knowing all that, Sara decided being with him
for however long would be worth the inevitable hurt.
Philosophy from the better-to-have-loved-and-lost
school of romance.

As soon as she made the decision, the unbearable
tension that had gripped her for days loosened its hold
to be replaced by a much more pleasant tension. It was
no longer a matter of if, but when and how. She drew a
deep breath.

"Well, well." Hayden turned and gave Sara a sharp
look.

Kayla and Amber shrieked and opened the door,
both talking at once. "Sara! We saw you on the TV!
Simon said he could find you and he did! Isn't this the
coolest? They've got drinks and hot dogs and nachos!
Come on in!" Kayla pulled on one hand and Amber
pulled on the other.

Sara laughed. It would be easier to resent Kayla if
Sara didn't recognize so much of herself at that age in
her. As the girls took her over to the nacho bar, Sara
looked up and saw Joanna watching her. Now *there*
was someone to resent. Someone Sara suspected had
more than a stepmotherly interest in Simon.

There were a couple more families of people from
Simon's division. Everybody was introduced to every-

body and in the process, the Glasgow men revealed Sara's return visit to the Stratford Oaks.

She'd pay for that later, she figured. But on the positive side, she introduced Missy and Hayden to Joanna, "Simon's stepmother." She did enjoy that.

Shortly after, Hayden murmured in her ear, "So it's a work night after all," and switched to full company marketing mode as she flirted with and charmed the men from Glasgow.

Missy, with a gentle, "Leave Joanna and the other women to me," practiced playing corporate wife.

Kayla and Amber shoved a hot dog at Sara, and then went to watch the game outside the box with three other kids.

Which left Sara standing next to Simon.

"Hello." His voice rumbled through her in a way no man's voice had ever rumbled.

"Hi."

How soon could she get him alone? How soon?

AT LEAST she was still speaking to him. Since their awkward coffee a couple of days ago, Simon had found Sara in his thoughts more often than not. He'd wanted another chance with her, but wasn't certain of the best way to approach her. Dazzling her with a big check hadn't done it, not that he would have liked her very much if it had.

He still thought the jazz brunch was a good idea, but he felt an intermediate step was needed, say one in which she actually conversed with him in more than one-sentence bursts.

He'd been thinking about her when Kayla and Amber had screamed that they'd seen her on the TV screen. He'd caught a quick glimpse, then a longer one of Hayden and had taken a chance.

Kayla had been terribly impressed with him. Joanna had eyed him speculatively. The Glasgow bunch had brightened and he, well, he'd looked on Sara's presence at this game as a gift.

Now, how to make the most of it?

He'd have to tread carefully to avoid offending her. Slow and steady won the race and all that.

But he didn't want to go slow and he certainly wasn't steady. He wanted her alone. More importantly, he wanted mutual wanting. And he wanted it pretty damn quick.

She had to know he found her attractive. The whole room probably knew, because he couldn't stop looking at her.

The sliding glass doors opened. "Sara!" Kayla shrieked. Kayla shrieked all conversation these days. "Come watch with us!"

"Let me eat my hot dog first," Sara said.

"'Kay." Kayla shoved the doors shut.

Simon liked the way Sara casually interacted with Kayla and her friend. She didn't make too much of her the way a couple of women had and neither did she talk awkwardly to her the way some adults did. And Kayla seemed genuinely glad to see her.

Joanna...he didn't care what Joanna thought.

"Would you like something to drink with your hot dog?" he asked Sara.

"Maybe later." She gingerly took a bite.

It drew attention to her mouth and it was probably best that Simon's attention not be on her mouth just now. He looked away. "I'm glad the weather is sunny. I enjoy the games when the stadium roof is retracted."

She nodded and swallowed.

He'd now exhausted the weather and the stadium as conversational topics. He couldn't stand the awkwardness between them one more instant. Not feeling the way he did.

As Sara raised the hot dog to her mouth, Simon took her arm and drew her over to the refrigerator away from the others.

"Do I make you uncomfortable?" Might as well go for it.

She looked up at him with an unreadable expression. "In a way." Just before she stared down at her hot dog, he caught the upward curve of her mouth.

Maybe he still had a shot. Opening the refrigerator, he took two bottles of water and opened one for her without asking. "In what way?"

She set the hot dog down on the counter and took the water. "You...you're...I owe you so many favors."

"What favors?" He got the impression that she'd been thinking of something else. He'd certainly been thinking of something else.

"Well, it started with fixing the photocopier, then you rescued that paper—"

"And then you saved my evening with Kayla, so we're even."

"Had a good time doing it, too." She smiled and he was encouraged. "We may have been even then, but you also got me into the Stratford Oaks, followed by the gym, *and* you gave me a huge check for the ballet. I can't ever repay you."

She felt in his debt. Not good. "I don't want to be repaid!" He lowered his voice. "I hope you don't feel that I expect you—" the memory of their kiss—his kiss—at the gym burned in his mind "—that you feel pressured to—"

"No." Shaking her head, she touched his arm. "That's not your style. And, by the way, you have a great..." her gaze dropped to his mouth then met his eyes "...style."

There was a humming in his ears and a distinct stirring elsewhere. His lungs felt tight.

She dropped her hand. "It makes me uncomfortable to have you think I need rescuing all the time."

"It's part of your charm."

Sara made a face. "Personally, I do not find incompetence at all charming."

"There's a difference between incompetence and needing a little help now and then."

"Right."

"For instance, I need help feeding a couple of cats next week."

She blinked up at him. "Tell me more about these cats."

"They belong to my neighbor, who's on a cruise. I hadn't anticipated leaving town while she was away, but..." he gestured to the Glasgow men, who appeared to be enthralled with Hayden. "It looks like I'm headed to Glasgow at the end of the week. Mind you, I'm not complaining, but I do need to find someone to feed her cats. I'd ask Kayla, but she'd have to make her own way over to the building, which would inconvenience Joanna and I'd rather not do that."

Sara was smiling, actually smiling.

He smiled, too. "So, could I inconvenience you instead?"

"I am delighted to be inconvenienced."

"Really?"

"I'm thrilled to find a way to repay you."

And he was thrilled that she was thrilled. "Great." His relief was enormous and it had nothing to do with finding someone to feed the cats. "I'll drop a key by tomorrow. Do you want to sit and watch the game?" That was smoothly added, if he did say so himself.

"I guess that *is* why we're here."

"Come on then. The view is great. You can see the skyline from here, too." Simon steered Sara to the bar seats behind the windows facing the field. He gave a passing thought to his clients, but they seemed fine with Hayden. Though he'd never worked directly with her, he knew her to be a consummate professional in spite of her flamboyant personal life. He caught her eye and indicated the game in progress. She gave a quick nod. Joanna was chatting with the other women. Kayla and Amber were watching from the two rows outside the suite.

Everyone was taken care of.

Now he could turn all his attention to Sara.

IT WAS THE CATS that did it. If she'd had the slightest hesitation about going for it with Simon, that obliterated it.

Sara wasn't a cat person, but how could she resist a man who fed his neighbor's cats?

It said a lot about his character. It occurred to Sara that, until now, she might have slept with a guy before knowing anything about his character—or the fact that he didn't have one.

Now that she knew Simon had character, she was ready for more.

She could hardly wait. Unfortunately, with all the people around, it looked as though she would have to.

"Are you a baseball fan?" he asked.

"I don't know yet."

He laughed. "That's an interesting way to put it."

"Well, I never really thought about it. My family wasn't into sports, but lately I've been trying out some new things." Maybe Simon would take the hint that she was willing to try out some new men, too. "I was in a rut."

"I commend you for doing something about it. Some people never take that initiative."

Sara didn't want to be commended unless it involved having Simon's lips a lot closer to her than they were at the moment.

In all fairness to him, he couldn't know that she'd just now changed her strategy of avoiding him to whatever the extreme opposite of avoiding him was. She had to maneuver the conversation to a more personal level.

Simon beat her to it. "Sara, when I asked you if I made you uncomfortable, the way you answered made me think there was something else you wanted to say."

"Hmm."

"Is that a yes?"

She crossed her legs and leaned her elbow on the chair arm between them. "It was an hmm."

"Define 'hmm.'" He leaned on his elbow, too.

Simon this close really ratcheted up the lustometer. He was looking at her in that way he had that connected the two of them and excluded the rest of the universe.

"Hmm means extremely attractive men make me uncomfortable."

"And are you uncomfortable now?"

Honestly. She could just wrap herself in his voice and fall into those eyes. "Extremely uncomfortable."

He leaned infinitesimally closer. "Anything I can do?"

"Oh, yes."

But did they get around to discussing details? No. Why?

"You two look very cozy all alone over here."

Joanna. That was why.

To Sara's utter disgust, she flinched when she heard Joanna's voice. Joanna must have seen, of course.

Simon didn't flinch. In fact he didn't move at all until she sat herself down on the bar stool on his other side. She chattered about the game, asking questions that forced Simon to answer, commented on the people, hopped up and got the snack tray and managed to get in a dig at Sara, "Have some nachos. You look like a girl with a good appetite."

If Sara had been Hayden, she would have answered, "I do have a big appetite, but not for nachos" and looked significantly at Simon.

But Sara wasn't Hayden, so she ate some nachos.

At one point, Joanna actually chided Simon for ignoring his hosting duties.

He gave Sara an apologetic smile. "I should make the rounds again."

Don't let yourself be manipulated by her she wanted to say, but frankly, it wasn't looking good for the home team.

Kayla and Amber saw her sitting by herself and gestured for her to come and sit with them.

Sure, why not? Sara got three soft drinks from the fridge and slid open the doors. It was noisier out here—closer to the sights and sounds and smells of the game.

"We've got peanuts." Amber showed her the bags.

"I like peanuts." Sara handed them each a soft drink,

crunched over the peanut shells on the concrete floor and sat down.

Even though Simon only poked his head out once or twice, Sara had a pretty good time. She cracked open peanut shells and tossed them at the heads of the boys in front of them, giggling along with Kayla and Amber. To make up for it, she put together a plate of snacks and brought it out to the boys, which they thought was cool. During the seventh-inning stretch, she reconnoitered with Missy and Hayden.

"Ladies, I think I'm about to find out what a Scotsman wears under his kilt." Hayden waggled her fingers at one of the Glasgow men.

"I'm sorry about letting Joanna get away," Missy said in a low tone. "We'll talk later, but Sara, you need to watch your back with that one. She's got her eye on Simon."

"I—" Sara started to protest that it was nothing to her, but gave up. "Okay. Thanks."

"I'll try to get her to sit with us again. Hang in there." Missy patted her arm and drifted back to the wives.

And Hayden was over there doing hostess duties so Simon wouldn't be so tied down.

To heck with her budget, Sara owed them lunch tomorrow.

Then the game was over and everybody cleared out. Sara tried to hang back, but Joanna and the girls had Simon surrounded.

They were all the way down the corridor when Kayla gasped, "I can't find my cell phone!"

"Did you bring it with you?" Joanna asked.

"It must have fallen out of my purse." She held up a tiny thing that didn't look large enough to hold a cell phone.

"I'll go back and look for it," Simon offered. "Go on ahead."

The elevator doors opened, but not everyone could get in. Somehow, Missy herded Joanna and the girls inside and Hayden and a couple of men filled it the rest of the way up. As the doors closed, they both looked significantly at Sara.

Right. Message received. She slipped away from the rest of the group and headed back to the club box.

She was going to be alone with Simon. Alone, alone, alone. Sara started jogging. She wouldn't have much time. She'd have to use it wisely.

But how? What was she going to do? Burst in and say, "'We're alone! Have your way with me'?" Efficient, but kind of tacky.

She reached the club box before she'd thought of exactly what to say or how to say it.

Simon was squatting down looking beneath the seats and didn't see her until she slid open the glass doors. He looked up, and honestly, she had to grip the railing to keep her knees from buckling. He just looked so good and they were just so alone—not counting the few thousand people still streaming toward the exits.

But they were far away. In this area, she and Simon were alone.

He stood. "Sara."

They looked at each other. Sara felt feelings that had been simmering all evening come to a full boil. She was ready to fling herself into his arms when, eyes never wavering from hers, he began steadily climbing the steps toward her.

"D-did you find the cell phone?" Not the best opening for seduction, but who cared.

"Right here." He held it up and continued to climb the steps to where she was standing.

Without pausing he reached for her, drew her to his chest and angled his head.

"Good," she whispered just before his mouth captured hers in a hungry kiss.

No, *this* was good. This was great. She'd ached for this, for his arms around her and his mouth on hers. Just to be touching him. It was almost too much. Desire bloomed from deep within her, deeper than ever before. She clutched at his shoulders and kissed him back for all she was worth.

He gripped her tightly and she stood on her toes to get even closer to him.

"Sara..." He dragged kisses along her jaw to the hollow beneath her ear. "So soft. So sweet."

When his mouth claimed hers again, it was for a deep and thorough kiss.

That software guy had nothing on Simon. Simon kissed with a breathtaking intensity that blotted everything else from Sara's mind. She almost forgot where she was, but not who she was with.

The ride in the Rolls had begun.

Simon ran his hands over her back, then cupped her head, his fingers playing with her hair. "You have no idea how long I've wanted this."

"You've kissed me before."

"But you never kissed me back."

"If you'll recall, I didn't have much of a chance." She nipped his lower lip. "I'm liking my chances now."

"And I'm liking them, too." He drew a deep breath and rested his forehead against hers as he traced light circles in the small of her back. "Which is why I have to stop kissing you now."

"I'll be uncomfortable if you stop kissing me now."

"Keep talking like that and I'll remember that there's a sofa just on the other side of that sliding glass door."

"Last one there's a rotten egg."

"You deserve better." He dropped a quick, hard kiss on her forehead and deliberately set her from him. "And don't look at me like that."

"I don't know how else to look at you." She was dizzy with first-real-kiss lust. Every nerve was humming with desire and the heady knowledge that he was as affected as she was.

Simon sucked in his breath through his teeth. "Sara, tonight I—"

And then his attention was caught and held by something over her shoulder.

Sara didn't want to turn around and see who was there, but of course she did.

Joanna stared at them through the open glass doors, her face expressionless.

So she'd seen them. Big deal, right? Sara turned back to Simon, trying to guess his thoughts, but his face was now as closed as Joanna's.

Sara was caught in the middle of some long history. The best thing she could do was stay quiet.

"I came back to help you look for Kayla's cell phone," Joanna said.

How lame. At least Sara hadn't pretended any such thing. Silently, Simon held up the phone.

Sara was trying not to look on this as a test.

"Thank you." Joanna held out her hand for it, forcing Simon to climb up to her. She turned to leave, but Simon stepped back down to Sara.

"They're holding the elevator for us," Joanna said.

"Why would they do that?" Simon asked. "It's a long walk."

"Politeness."

"I see." Simon lazily linked his fingers through Sara's and headed up the stairs with her.

Whoo-hoo! Score one for Sara. Except the long icy look Joanna gave her made it a hollow victory.

8

"SHE JUST STOPPED the elevator and got right out!" Missy was aghast at Joanna's escape. "She abandoned her child and everything!"

"So what did she see?" Hayden eyed Sara over her glass of iced green tea.

Sara had bought them lunch the next day. They weren't at their usual spot, but at a Chinese restaurant down in the tunnels. "Depends on when Joanna got there."

The other two just looked at her.

"Okay, he kissed me."

Hayden and Missy high-fived each other.

"I am dying to know how it was unless it wasn't any good. Then lie because I don't want that particular fantasy shot to hell."

"Hayden, I'm not sure I want you fantasizing about Simon that way."

"I'm going to, so get over it. Spill."

Sara closed her eyes. "Oh. My. God."

Hayden and Missy squealed.

"It was one of those kisses that is definitely going somewhere. But unfortunately it couldn't go anywhere just then."

"So just when?" Hayden asked.

This was the tricky part because, frankly, Sara had neither seen nor heard from Simon since last night. "Soon."

"How soon?" Hayden pressed.

"I don't know, okay?" Sara wasn't exactly worried yet, but there were a few niggling doubts.

"I knew it!" Missy snapped her chopsticks apart. She was the only one trying to use them. "That Joanna has something to do with it."

Sara really hated to think that Joanna had that much influence on Simon.

"He doesn't seem like the kiss-and-run type," Missy added.

"Not when there's more to be had." Hayden snickered.

"Don't be vulgar."

"Missy, sex isn't vulgar."

"I know, but the way you talk about it sometimes is."

"Hey!" Sara snapped her fingers to interrupt them. "I'll see Simon when he brings me the key."

Missy's eyes widened. "To his home?"

"No. I'm feeding his neighbor's cats."

They both looked at her. "Why?" Hayden asked.

"Because they need to be fed and he's leaving for Glasgow at the end of the week."

"Hmm," they both said.

"A loss of momentum this early in a relationship is not good," Missy said.

"But absence makes the heart grow fonder," Hayden quoted. "And she can have more time to prepare."

"Wait a minute. I don't think relationship is the right word here." Sara needed to let them know her immediate goal had changed. She wasn't sure how Missy would take it. "I'm just...just going for a ride in the Rolls."

"Not this again." Missy used her chopstick to stab a piece of chicken.

"All it means is that he's not a long-term prospect because of his sister and his stepmother." It helped to think of Joanna that way.

"Stepmother, oh please." Missy abandoned her chopsticks. "The first thing she did was tell us all that she never considered herself Simon's stepmother. And we were all, well, duh, you're like his age. And then we had to hear how close they'd become since his father had died and how good he was with his sister."

Sara was glad she hadn't had to hear it.

Missy dipped her egg roll in some sticky red sauce. "It's probably just as well that you don't have any expectations because that woman has her hooks into him but good."

"Sara can handle her," Hayden said loyally.

"Hmph," Missy said around a mouthful of eggroll.

"I understand his priorities. They come first." Sara sounded very mature.

And maybe a little whiny.

"Are you going to eat any more of the lo mein?" Hayden asked. When Sara shook her head, she drew it toward her. "When I find myself in such a situation, I just make it more fun to be with me than with them."

"They interrupt."

"So make him want to turn off his cell phone."

"You know, I don't see why he can't be marriage material." Missy toyed with the fortune cookies before deciding on one. "Sara has to overcome the wicked stepmother and the bratty half sister either way."

"Excellent point." Hayden gestured to Sara's hot and sour soup, now just warm and sour. "Are you going to eat that?"

"Yes." She didn't have much of an appetite today, though. She took a mouthful of soup.

"I think Sara should postpone her tryst—"

"Tryst! What century are you from, honey?"

Missy exhaled forcefully. "I think she should avoid boinking him until after he gets back from Glasgow. She should welcome him back with a home-cooked meal and provide a haven from the stresses of the modern work world."

"Watch out. She's quoting from her *Stepford Wives for Dummies* book."

"I just think that it couldn't hurt for Sara to demonstrate her domestic potential."

Sara gave a warning look to Hayden, who looked as though she was about to deliver one of her pithy put-downs. "A dinner might not be a bad idea. Simon once asked me if I could cook."

"There you are." Missy looked pleased. "While he's gone, we'll plan a menu and you can practice on us."

"That's all very well and good, but at this point, Simon isn't thinking about her cooking abilities." Hayden gave a catlike smile. "Sara, all you have to do is wrap yourself in Saran Wrap and a fur coat and pay a little after-hours visit to his office. I guarantee you that you'll have his uninterrupted attention for as long as you want it."

Missy had her mouth open. "Saran Wrap?"

"Men go nuts, I'm telling you. And it's fabulous for a first time because your boobs aren't sagging and your butt and thighs and stomach are compressed and sculpted. No jiggling. There you are, gleaming as you slowly open the coat. And all that carefully arranged perfection is his first impression of you. It's the image that'll stick with him no matter what he thinks he sees later."

There was silence, then Missy ventured a question. "They have red, blue and green plastic wrap. Do you think—"

"Clear."

"Oh. Okay."

Well. "On that note..." Sara reached for a fortune cookie, cracked it open, read the fortune and burst into laughter.

"What does it say?" Hayden snatched it out of her unresisting fingers, read it and flung it down.

Missy retrieved it. "'You will receive wise counsel from an elder.'" She laughed. "Elder. Oh, that's good."

Sara was still laughing to herself as she made her way back to her cubicle.

Laughing until she saw the white envelope sitting on her desk.

She opened the envelope and a key fell out, along with a sheet of lined notebook paper with handwriting on it. A smaller note was also in the envelope.

Simon's initials were stamped at the top of the paper.

"Sara, I'll be out of the office until after my trip. I've had to take a couple of personal days to drive Kayla and Joanna to visit one summer camp near Austin and another one near Dallas. Kayla is lukewarm about going and Joanna felt a united front from us would reassure her."

Sara stopped reading to admire Joanna's tactics. Maybe Saran Wrap and a fur coat wasn't overkill after all.

"I know you understand that I wouldn't leave now if it weren't important. The opportunity arose quickly because Kayla is off from school due to a teacher's seminar and apparently waiting until I returned from this trip wasn't feasible since camp reservations fill up so quickly. I'll be flying to Glasgow out of Dallas, but as soon as I can, I'll call you."

She'd heard that before.

"Here are the instructions for feeding Mrs. Galloway's cats as well as a copy of her key. I still have one. Just in case."

Just in case what? Just in case she accidentally on purpose dropped it down the garbage disposal? No. She wouldn't do that to a couple of helpless kitties.

"Thanks for understanding, Sara. Uncomfortably yours, Simon."

She smiled a little at the "uncomfortably."

So round one was to Joanna. But Sara had not yet begun to fight.

She wondered if she could find any used faux furs online.

OVER THE NEXT couple of days, she planned a dozen menus, winnowed them down and discussed food strategies with Missy and Hayden. Finally, she decided on the winning dinner: salmon mousse and champagne, grilled filet mignon—because Hayden had insisted that she feed Simon beef—baked potato, strawberry, walnut and mesclun salad—to demonstrate that she could be traditional and innovative—and bread pudding because it was soft and warm and sweet and suggestive—and because it could be made the night before.

"That's a heavy meal," Hayden commented. "We don't want to weigh him down. Ditch the bread pudding and go with a chocolate mousse."

"But she's having salmon mousse to start. The textures are too similar."

"Then serve him ice cream. Men like ice cream." Hayden grinned. "And have you ever kissed while eating ice cream?"

Sara could tell Missy was thinking about it. "But the beauty of bread pudding is that if you don't get around to eating it, you bring it out the next morning and call it a French toast casserole."

Hayden gave her an admiring look. "Why, Missy. I am so shocked."

Sara decided to go with the bread pudding and buy some chocolate chunk ice cream to keep in reserve.

A couple of nights later, she invited Hayden and Missy over to her apartment for a trial run. It was a good thing because the mousse was runny, so Sara changed her appetizer to salmon spread, but everything else was going fine and she felt reasonably confident that she could cook the meal for Simon.

Now, Missy and Hayden in her apartment was something else. They prowled around and checked out her CD collection, which wasn't large or current. "I mostly listen to the radio," Sara explained from the kitchen.

"Let's get her some better CDs," Hayden said to Missy, who was following her around making notes.

They made Sara nervous, but that still was no excuse for the runny salmon.

"Definitely," Missy said. "We should also do some romantic feng shui or something."

Hayden bounced on the couch. "This is not the most inviting piece of furniture."

"Well, sorry. It's a sofa bed," Sara told her.

"They're never as comfortable as regular sofas," Hayden said knowledgeably.

"Pillows and a nice soft throw," Missy wrote.

"Candles," Hayden said.

"Fresh flowers," Missy added.

"New sofa," Hayden snuck in.

"Oh, come on! I can't afford all that!" Sara brought out the runny mouse and some champagne.

Missy checked the label. "Go for Veuve Clicquot."

"Do you know how expensive that stuff is?"

"Yes. I've been researching champagnes for my wedding reception. It's so worth it."

"This is a Rolls we're talking about, kiddo," Hayden reminded her. "Missy, let's check out the bedroom."

While they did so, Sara sat on her hard, uncomfortable sofa, drank her cheap champagne, dipped crackers in what was now salmon soup, and told herself that it would all be worth it.

Missy and Hayden came out of the bedroom. "Emergency shopping trip tomorrow at lunch," Missy said. "I can't believe you haven't discovered the joy of six-hundred thread count sheets."

"And honey, the stuffed animals have got to go."

Sara poured herself more champagne. "I thought they added a touch of whimsy. Cows and sheep and clouds?"

Hayden and Missy shook their heads.

Hayden gave her a stern look. "Tell me you don't have whimsical lingerie, as well."

"Cow pajamas," Sara mumbled with cracker in her mouth.

"You won't be wearing pajamas. You need a silk robe. Missy, make a note."

"Already did."

"I have a nice, big, fluffy, white terry cloth robe."

"Excellent. You'll be lending that to Simon."

AND THEN there were the cats. Sara was not a cat person and they sensed that. Each day after work, she let herself into the huge penthouse apartment in one of Houston's few high-rises and the cats hid from her. They were named Tony and Cleo—how original—and she never got close enough to figure out which was Tony and which was Cleo.

She plopped her purse on the counter and shook the bag of dry cat food. There was a complicated rotation of foods for the cats. And today, oh, what fun, today was litter box day. In spite of all the apparent advances in the litter box field, automatic litter boxes could only be so automatic.

Sara cleaned the bowls in the kitchen, the only evidence—other than the litter box—that the cats were actually in the apartment.

"Hey, Tony, hey Cleo, it's me, your gullible food slave. Why don't you guys come out so I can see you and I won't have to hunt you down just to see if you're still alive? You know I'm going to and you know I'll leave right after, so come on. Give me a break."

She wanted a break in another area, too. Simon hadn't called her. Sure, he was overseas, but come on. It wouldn't hurt to e-mail—yes, it would be forever in the company records, but surely he could think of something innocuous to say just to make contact.

He'd been gone for over a week including the bogus

trip to check out summer camps. He wasn't scheduled to be back until next Monday. Maybe he'd call her before then.

No, she hadn't given him her phone number, but it was in the book. He could find it if he wanted. And after she'd invested in champagne and hideously expensive, but oh-so-luxurious sheets which spoiled her for any other kind, he'd *better* call.

Sara finished putting out the food and water and emptying the litter box waste receptacle, then went looking for the cats. She checked under the sumptuous sofa, a favorite spot, but no cats. Instead of heading for the bedroom, their other favorite spot, she sat on the sofa and sank into the cushions. Oh, yeah. This was one comfortable sofa. It was long, too. Sara stretched out and lifted her arms as though encouraging Simon to lean over her and cover her body with his. Bliss.

This was the kind of sofa Hayden had been talking about. Unfortunately, it was way too big for Sara's modest apartment. But they had found some cushy pillows and a chenille throw that had softened Sara's couch. They'd made her buy other accessories at the home store and then Missy had made her take something called a "scent personality test" so she'd pick the right candle scent.

Sara realized that Simon was the first man she'd been interested in who would appreciate cushy pillows and chenille throws and scented candles. She liked that about him.

What she didn't like about him was that he hadn't

called. Maybe there would be a message on her machine today. The sooner she got out of this place, the sooner she could go check.

She went into the bedroom with its high-thread-count sheets, which she recognized now that she was a sheet connoisseur, and lifted the dust ruffle to check under the bed. A pair of cat eyes blinked back at her. But just one pair of cat eyes.

"Hi, Tony or Cleo. Where's your cohort in crime?" Now that she'd located one cat, she'd have to watch that it didn't escape and get mistaken for the other.

Sara looked under all the furniture, but didn't find the other cat. She didn't feel comfortable snooping in a stranger's home, but she did want to find that cat.

She went back into the kitchen and checked the pantry, just in case the cat had gone in there when she wasn't looking. No cat. She closed the door firmly. She checked all the other rooms again and was back in the bedroom when she noticed the closet door was ajar.

A spurt of adrenaline shot through her, because she knew that she hadn't opened any closet doors today and that they'd been closed every other time she'd played hunt-the-cat. Had someone broken in? Was a burglar hiding in the closet?

Sara's mouth went dry until she remembered that the maid had come today. She must not have closed the door all the way.

"You naughty cat." Sara opened the closet door and was at first stunned by the sheer size of the space. "What is this? Another spare bedroom?"

She turned on the lights and saw a professionally organized closet with an electronic clothing rack. Sara flipped a switch and Mrs. Galloway's clothes began to march around and back up near the ceiling. "Wow." Another switch worked a rotating purse and shoe rack.

"I am so cleaning out my closet when I get home."

And then Sara stopped the moving clothes. Not one, not two, but three fur coats swung softly before her. At first glance she knew that at least two were fake, or somebody needed to be held accountable for the purple and red fur. The third one was long and black and had it been real, it would have been in a cold-storage vault instead of here in the closet in a cloth bag with a little window on it.

She heard a sound and ducked beneath the coats to find a cat, a cat who had made a very nice cashmere nest for itself.

"You are so busted." Sara tried to retrieve the sweater.

"Rowr!" The cat swiped at her and she jumped back. The cats had been declawed, but they hadn't been detoothed.

"Calm down. It's only me." Maybe if she hung around the cat would get hungry enough to come out of the closet by itself and Sara could shut the door. She wasn't too pleased that it had probably ruined a cashmere sweater on her watch, but that was between Mrs. Galloway and her maid.

Sara crawled back out from beneath the coats and then got an idea, an idea that might not have seemed so great if she'd stopped to think about it. But there were these coats. And Sara was all alone except for the cats and she really did want to get the cat out of the closet before she left, which meant she had to hang around.

There was Saran Wrap in the pantry. She'd seen it. She had practiced cooking dinner, it made sense to practice the plastic wrap/fur coat scenario. Perfect sense.

Sara gingerly took down the long black coat and unzipped the cloth bag. The first thing she noticed was how utterly soft and luxurious it was. The second thing she noticed was the PETA label embroidered in red in the collar and down one side of the lining. The other label had some politically correct babble about recreating the elegance of fur in a kinder world.

Fake. She got the message already.

Sara lay the coat bag on the bed and got the plastic wrap from the kitchen. Feeling self-conscious, she undressed in the master bathroom where her naked self was reflected repeatedly.

Now. Where to start? She unrolled a length of plastic and wrapped it around herself like a towel and immediately knew that wasn't the look Hayden had in mind.

Sara took the whole roll out of the carton. Starting beneath her left arm, she moved the roll across her breasts and behind her back, where it fell to the white tiled floor.

She bent to pick up the roll and parts of it stuck to itself.

Okay. Go around the back first. Sara pulled the plastic from itself and started again, this time with better luck. The results weren't as visually appealing as Hayden suggested they might be.

Naked, and trailing plastic wrap behind her, Sara used the bedroom phone to call Hayden.

"Hayden? This is Sara. Look, the plastic wrap thing—how are you supposed to get it on?"

There was a short silence. "Where are you?"

"The cat lady's house. She's got a fur coat and I thought I'd practice."

"Is Simon there with you?"

"Of course not!"

"Is anyone there with you?"

"Just a couple of scaredy cats. Ha ha."

"It helps to have another person."

"There isn't anybody else. My boobs look horrible."

"Lay down on the bed. You want gravity to work with you here. Also, position yourself before you wrap."

"Okay. Hayden, how much am I wrapping? Do I wrap my legs together or separately? How far down?"

"Do you want to be able to walk?"

"I guess that would be helpful."

"You have a choice—miniskirt length, if there won't be a fat roll midway to your knees, or try a crisscross style."

"Plastic wrap has styles?"

"Just experiment."

"Okay."

"Sara—don't forget to pull tight."

"Gotcha." She hung up the phone and positioned herself on the bed.

Wrapping herself was a little easier from a prone position, but Sara was getting a real workout. When she finished and stood, sweat trickled beneath the plastic.

She wrapped her legs separately down to her knees, but it was hard to bend to get lower. When she did this the next time, she was going to start with her leg and wrap up, so that little rolls of fat didn't collect down at her knees. Gravity. Must work with gravity.

She left her arms bare because by this time she was exhausted and figured that any man faced with a naked plastic-wrapped woman wouldn't be looking at her arms.

Sara walked into the bathroom to see how she looked. The whole effect wasn't bad—as though she had on a clear, strapless capri pant suit.

But was it sexy?

It was loud. Maybe that was what the fur coat was for—to deaden the sound.

Next time, she should try for less plastic to cut down on some of the folds. It might be cooler, too, since she'd already noticed little areas getting fogged with heat.

The bathroom was too hot, that was it. Sara crackled her way back into the bedroom and slipped into the coat for the full effect.

For a moment, she forgot that she was naked under the coat and just stared at herself in the full-length mirror on the closet door. Wow. She was beginning to get the coat thing.

She vamped a little, channeling her inner vixen, letting the collar slide off her shoulder. Then she let it slide off her other shoulder. Turning, she loosened it more so that she could see the fur against her bare back.

There was something about the deep black that brought out the creaminess in her skin. It might even be better without the plastic, she mused.

Unlike *some* people, she didn't have a whole lot of sagging going on.

Slowly, Sara turned back around until she faced herself in the mirror. Trying to see herself through Simon's eyes, she dropped the coat to her waist.

Too fast. Hitching it up again, she made it slowly slide down her arms, one hand clutching it just beneath her exposed breasts.

Yowser.

She was so going on a thrift shop hunt for a fur coat. She threw back her shoulders and practiced various expressions and poses, ultimately simply staring, trying to imitate Simon's intensity.

And that was the one that finally got her. She stared at herself the way she imagined he would, taking in the fur against her skin, the way the plastic wrap covered all, yet revealed everything. Her breasts, slightly flattened yet lush, begging to be unwrapped.

Sara released the coat and it slithered to the floor.

Her breath quickened as she imagined Simon's would. He would want to touch her. Here...and there…Sara closed her eyes as a bead of sweat trickled between her breasts.

Okay, she was hot—on a couple of levels. The level she was concerned with was the one making the plastic wrap unstick.

She must have done something wrong. Impulsively, she picked up the phone and called Hayden again.

"What am I doing wrong?"

"What do you mean?"

"I'm so hot!"

"That's the idea, honey."

"Yeah, but I'm really hot. Sweating hot. It's not attractive."

"How long have you been wrapped up?"

"Since I called you last."

"You're probably using too much plastic wrap, or that coat is really thick."

"Both, I think. But this coat is something else. It's fake, but it's such a good fake she's got PETA stuff embroidered in it so the paint people won't get her. It looks like a full-length sable, or something like that."

"Hmm. They are the best."

Sara heard a noise. "I think that stupid cat is finally leaving the closet."

Then there was another noise. A horrible, terrible awful noise. A key-in-the-front-door noise. Her stomach clenched. "Oh, Hayden," she whispered. "Someone is coming in the door!"

9

OMIGOSHOMIGOSHOMIGOSH. She was naked in some-one else's apartment. And not just regular naked, but kinky naked. Kinky naked and trying on someone else's clothes.

Ignoring Hayden's alarmed questions sounding clearly through the receiver, Sara carefully hung up the phone. She heard the key turn in the lock, so the person coming in had to be either the owner—and how on earth was she supposed to explain what she was doing to the owner of the penthouse?—or the building super-intendent.

Or a burglar with a skeleton key.

She had a split second to decide what to do.

The coat. The coat was on the floor by the mirror and would be in sight of whoever it was. As the door opened, Sara scrambled around the bed as fast as she could, considering she was hampered by moist plastic wrap, and leaped for the coat.

Don't panic don't panic. Shrugging into the fur, she held her breath. If it was the super, he'd probably do whatever he was going to do and leave.

If it was the owner—oh, please, no—she should hear

sounds of luggage being dragged in, probably by another person.

If it was a burglar, she should call 9-1-1, but she wasn't near the phone, now, was she?

Her clothes were in the bathroom, on the other side of the cavernous master bedroom and she had to pass the open doorway to get there.

If she could get there, she could at least pretend she'd been using the bathroom. Or if she could get her clothes and dress in the closet, the cat could be her excuse and that would explain the coat. Somehow.

Nothing would explain the rumpled bed.

She held her breath, heart pounding, as the door closed. *Please, please, please, be the super.* Sara edged toward the closet and opened the door. She could hide inside. The thing was huge. Maybe she could grab on and ride the clothes train all the way to the ceiling.

She backed into the closet, felt something brush against her ankles and heard a yowl as the stupid cat shot between her legs.

Okay. A distraction could be good. She got ready to run for the bathroom.

"Sara?" A voice. Male.

Simon.

She froze. That was Simon's voice. *Simon.* The same Simon who was supposed to be in Europe. And who clearly was not in Europe, because he was here, in his neighbor's apartment.

How did he know she was here?

Her purse was on the counter, that's how.

"Sara, where are you?" She could hear him moving.

She could lock herself in the bathroom, but that wouldn't explain what she was doing with the coat.

What she was doing with the coat. She'd been practicing. For Simon. And here he was. Talk about a little sexy serendipity.

Should she? Could she? Once he got over the surprise, he wouldn't quibble about the details, would he?

Sara wrapped the coat tightly around her. It was a furnace inside this coat. She'd discovered the cure for freezing to death. Furs and Saran Wrap. Nobody would ever be cold again. Siberia could be a paradise. When she got out of this, she'd write the president.

Stop. Concentrate.

"Sara?" His voice was much closer.

Okay, she was going to have to answer him. She walked to the doorway of the bedroom. "Simon." She was trying for a low purr, but got a cracked squeak.

He turned around—and was holding the damn cashmere sweater cat.

Oh, but the delight that spread across his face did bolster her self-esteem. "There you are."

"Yes, here I am." She cleared her throat and stepped into the living room. "I've been trying to get that cat out of the closet ever since I got here, and as soon as it hears you, it's out of there like a shot."

"You miss me, Cleo?" He scratched behind the cat's ears.

She purred and blinked at Sara.

Cleo, you slut.

Then Simon raised his eyes. Oh, that look. It was one of the sexiest things about him, the way he could look at her and make her think she was the only woman in the world. Make her think of the possibilities that came with being the only woman in the world in Simon's eyes.

It was addicting, that look. He was just laying it all out there, signaling his interest, making himself vulnerable, cutting through all the posturing men usually did.

Simon could seduce with just that look. It made a girl wonder what he could do with his hands, his mouth and other pertinent parts of his anatomy—particularly to a girl naked beneath a fur coat.

He didn't seem to notice the coat. Maybe she could bluff her way through this.

Sweat trickled down her legs. "You're back early."

His fingers had stopped scratching Cleo's ears and the cat jumped down, streaking toward the kitchen. "I worked like a madman so I could get back to you."

Oh, wow. Exactly the right words. Words that slammed into her and revved up her idling motor.

"I've just come from the airport." He was dressed in a suit that looked nothing like a suit that had been worn on a transatlantic flight, but his hair was endearingly wavy, not tamed with its usual ruthlessness.

His eyes, though tired, had lost none of their intensity. "You didn't answer when I called your home, so I took a chance that you'd be here."

"And here I am." Hadn't she already said that?

"Yes." It was almost a whisper, a whisper that curled around her heart.

Shouldn't somebody be kissing somebody?

Simon's expression was full of such intense longing and desire that it filled her with an answering need. And yet, he stood there, his hands loosely at his sides.

Sweat trickled beneath her breasts and she realized that her arms—her fur-covered arms—were crossed over them in the classic defensive position. "I suppose you're wondering about the coat."

"No."

"Houston gets a little crazy with the air conditioning..." He'd said "no."

And that was the moment she fell in love with him. She was standing in his neighbor's apartment wearing her fur coat—naked, and he didn't even know it. He'd worked himself past exhaustion just to be with her and now stood there, barely holding himself in check because he was waiting for the tiniest little signal from her and she'd given him nothing. Had she said she was glad to see him? Had she smiled at him? Told him she'd missed him? Had she in any way indicated that she wanted him?

No.

And he wanted her. This fabulous hunk of a man wanted *her*. Fiercely. She had no doubt of that. But he must doubt her.

It was time to remove all doubt. It was time to remove the coat.

She took a step farther into the room. "I've been thinking of you."

A muscle twitched in the side of his jaw.

"And Hayden, well..." This was harder than she thought. She just couldn't quite get there. She needed some intro music, or something.

"I haven't been thinking of Hayden at all."

"Good—I mean, sometimes Hayden has some good ideas." She tried for a sophisticated Hayden laugh and all she got was a nervous, breathy giggle. *So* sexy. She swallowed. "The coat was her idea." But that sounded like she was blaming Hayden. "She said that there was nothing like a fur coat to make a woman look alluring to a man."

Actually, Hayden hadn't said that, but it sounded like something she would say.

"You don't need a fur coat to be alluring. Take it off."

She shivered, even though she was hot. Maybe because she *was* hot. "Well, yes, well, um, there's more. Or less, actually." Where was her inner vixen? *Cleo* had more sensual moves than she did.

Simon took a step toward her. "Take the coat off." It was a rough whisper.

It wasn't a suggestion.

"I was just practicing that."

He'd started to take another step toward her when she let one side of the coat slip from her shoulder. Her naked shoulder. The slightly flushed—maybe a lot flushed—shoulder. The shoulder she thought looked so good against the fur.

Simon halted in midstep, his gaze trained on that very same shoulder.

So she showed him the other one.

His gaze flicked back and forth between the two as his brain attempted to process her naked shoulders. She wondered what he was thinking.

Quite frankly, it appeared as though he wasn't thinking at all. He looked as though he'd been smacked in the forehead with a two-by-four. She'd been going for more of a lustful reaction as opposed to stunned immobility.

Okay. She'd shown him two naked shoulders and that was it until she had some sort of encouragement. If he thought she was being ridiculous, she wanted to know and she wanted to know right now. Before the plastic came into view. Especially before what was under the plastic wrap came into view. But something was going to have to happen soon because she was so, so hot. She gave her inner vixen a couple of mental thwaps to revive her, in case she'd melted in the heat.

Her inner vixen told her to reveal some plastic-manufactured cleavage and call her again if anything developed.

Sara kind of thought something was developing even without revealing plastic cleavage because Simon's eyes had stopped darting between her shoulders and were fixed on her face with hopeful desperation.

Ooo, she could work with that. She tossed back her hair and gave a little shimmy that dropped the coat still farther, past the plastic line.

"S-Sara...are you wearing anything under that coat?"

Simon had stuttered. *Hey, hear that, vixen?* "Nothing of any consequence."

Sara took another step toward Simon, infinitely more confident now that her inner vixen was back on board. She met his gaze with a hot one of her own then looked down at herself, slowly lowering the coat. She glanced up to see that he was staring at the edges of the coat as they slipped lower.

Heart pounding, Sara felt the fur tickle over breasts, then fall away.

"My God." He gasped softly. "You—" He swallowed. "What...what is that..."

"I'm a package." Sara let the coat fall all the way to the floor. "Unwrap me."

His mouth opened and, tragically, wasn't anywhere near hers. "Y-you..." He swallowed and seemed to be trying to breathe. His mouth opened again.

The man seemed to be having a system meltdown. Ha. He was at her mercy.

Drawing a long, deep breath, Simon closed his eyes. "P-put the coat back on."

What? This wasn't what she wanted to hear. She wanted to hear "My God, you're beautiful," or "Where's the bed?" or "I am unworthy, but let me be your love slave."

He struggled to get out of his jacket. "Put this on."

Wrong. "I don't want to put on your jacket. I'm *hot*," she said deliberately.

"You don't understand." Simon looked desperate. And flushed.

"No, I don't."

"Thousands of years of civilization are draining from me as we speak. I'm turning into a Neanderthal. You don't have much time." He abandoned trying to get out of his jacket and bent to pick up the fur. He held it out to her. "If I get any closer, I'll drag you off to my lair."

All right. She could get into lair-dragging. Sara took the coat, but instead of putting it on, she tossed it aside. "Sounds good to me." And she took a step closer.

From this close, Simon did have a wild look in his eye. Without another word, he snatched up the coat and shrugged it around her shoulders, barely waiting for her to put her arms into the sleeves before grabbing her hand and heading for the door. He threw it open before she had a chance to pull the edges of the coat together with her free hand. Luckily, there was no one in the hall.

He was being quite the caveman and she loved it. Simon, the conservative, polite, thoughtful, contained man had been undone by passion. By desire for her. Tra la la.

"Simon?" She didn't have anything to say. She just wanted to see his expression when he looked at her.

His expression was hot and thrilling. He stopped

and yanked the edges of the fur closed and used her free hand to keep it closed.

"What? No kiss?"

"No."

She smiled to herself because she had to jog to keep up with him. He had started moving again. "But I want a kiss," she pouted. "Just a little one."

"No."

"Why not?"

"This is why not." Without warning, he pushed her against the wall, ground his pelvis against hers through the coat and crushed her mouth with his.

Yes. That was it. Exactly what she'd been waiting for, an explosion of raw passion. She'd tapped into the Simon reserves.

Sara opened her mouth as he plundered it and clung to him, knowing it wouldn't take much to send her over the edge.

The coat fell open and he thrust his knee between her legs.

Or tried to. The plastic was in the way.

A frustrated groan vibrated through her mouth as his hand moved against the plastic wrap seeking and finding her breast.

Sara inhaled because the muted sensations partially relieved one ache while fueling another.

More. She wanted more. She stood on tiptoe trying to fit Simon closer to her, trying to push aside the plastic wrap. She whimpered in frustration.

Simon made a strangled animal sound as he tugged

on the wrap at her breasts, then he raised his mouth from hers.

She looked into lust-crazed eyes and knew they mirrored her own. He bent his head and bit through the plastic, tearing it with his teeth.

She laughed, because it was so surreal and because she was drunk with desire.

She felt a rush of coolness as Simon freed her breasts, then a jolt of pleasure as he fastened his mouth on one.

His tongue touched her and she cried out. He lifted his head, but Sara moaned and pressed it back against her. She moaned again and one of his hands crept upward until his fingers gently pressed against her lips.

She bit him.

And he nipped her back.

"Simon!" Intense pleasure spiraled through her. She took his fingers in her mouth and sucked hard on them.

"Sara...Sara..."

Dimly, she became aware that she was making unfamiliar guttural noises and Simon had straightened and was trying to smother the sounds with his mouth.

His hands? Where were his hands and why weren't they on her?

She tore her mouth away to discover that he'd planted one hand against the hall corridor on either side of her shoulders.

"Simon!"

"Hush, Sara," he whispered from the crook of her neck.

"Don't stop, please! I was so close."

"I know. The entire state of Texas knows." He was dragging the breath into his lungs.

"Don't care." She licked his earlobe and he moved out of reach.

"We're in a public hallway. Someone could see us."

"They'd just be jealous."

"This isn't that kind of building." He pushed himself away from the wall and looked down at her. "You are devastatingly gorgeous." He gave his head a shake and pointed. "Coat. Closed. Now."

"Maybe I don't want to close the coat."

He closed it for her and pulled her along the hallway by it. "We have to get from here to my apartment four floors below. We will have to take the elevator. We will hope that we do not meet anyone on the way because you look like you've been doing exactly what you've been doing. And, by the way, it's a very good look for you. I plan to help you achieve that look as often as possible."

They'd made it to the elevators without encountering anyone else. He jabbed at the button and missed, which was pretty bad considering they were on the top floor and there was only the down button to push.

"See? Another thirty seconds, or twenty—fifteen tops—wouldn't have mattered," she pointed out and rubbed her bare foot against his calf.

"Sara."

"Just how many penthouses are there up here?"

"Four."

"And we know one of the occupants is on a cruise."

He didn't say anything, just stared at the elevator doors as though willing them to open.

Sara felt something float down her leg. "Simon, I'm trailing plastic wrap."

They both looked down as another loop of plastic wrap circled her legs. Sara bent to pick it up and her coat fell open.

Simon made a strangled noise. "Doesn't that thing have buttons?"

"A belt. I left it on the hanger."

He knelt down and tugged on the plastic wrap, rolling it up as though he were twining yarn. As the ball grew larger, Sara began to twirl around. And make little happy murmurings. "There is some seriously good rubbing going on here."

"Shh." Simon cast a frantic glance over his shoulder at the elevator. "I can hear it."

"The rubbing?"

"The *elevator*. Behave."

Sara stepped out of the last of the plastic and dragged the coat around herself as Simon gathered a beachball-sized armful of plastic wrap then stood up. He was still looking for some place to ditch it when the elevator doors opened.

Three people faced them. Sara tossed her hair and tried for a so-what-if-it's-May-and-I'm-wearing-a-fur-coat look. One woman stared hard at the coat and it occurred to Sara that if she lived in one of the penthouses on this floor, then there was a very good chance that she might be acquainted with Mrs. Galloway and might also be acquainted with Mrs. Galloway's furs.

"Good evening," Simon said in his most mellifluous voice and stood aside to let them exit the elevator.

He and Sara got in. She reached for him as the door closed.

"No." Very firmly he pointed to the other side of the elevator. "Over there. Stay."

"But why when I'm all completely naked under this coat?"

He clutched the plastic wrap ball to him. "Precisely because I am totally aware that you are completely naked under that coat."

From the far side of the not-very-big elevator, Sara let a sleeve slither off her shoulder. "Have I ever told you that elevator sex is one of my fantasies?"

He closed his eyes and the plastic wrap crackled. "No."

"Well, I'm telling you now." She took a step toward the control box.

"What are you doing?"

Sara held up her index finger in front of his tortured eyes. Slowly, she licked it, blew on it, then pointed it toward the emergency stop.

"No!" He lunged for her wrist and held it above her head. "I'm not proud of the hall incident—"

"I'm not proud either. I'm telling you, fifteen more seconds—"

"I have very little control left." The hot look he gave her didn't leave a doubt in her mind.

Oh, she loved the power she had over him. And she loved being out of the plastic wrap, too. Loved the feel of the satin lining and the turned in fur edges rubbing against her still sensitive breasts.

"Fifteen seconds," she whispered and reached out to stroke the long, hard length of him through his suit trousers. "A quickie. It'll take the edge off."

Simon shuddered, or rather the elevator shuddered to a halt.

Sara closed her coat as he positioned himself to one side, giving her a strained look of shocked lust. "You don't know what you're doing!" he ground out as the doors opened.

Two men in the middle of a conversation stepped on and absently acknowledged Simon, who smoothly stepped in front of Sara.

One of the men glanced her way, but his attention was captured by the other one.

"So you think ten o'clock?"

"Maybe we ought to try for lunch."

"Take up too much time."

"But if the meeting doesn't start until ten and we go over, then there's the awkwardness of ending at lunch time…"

Sara slipped her arm from the voluminous sleeve of the coat and reached through the opening toward Simon's rear and pinched.

A crackle of plastic was her only response.

She'd kind of pinched him hard. Maybe she should

rub it to make it better. So she did. She started with light circles, feeling his glutes tense beneath her hand.

She couldn't wait to see him naked. At the thought, her hand began a more up-and-down rhythmic motion.

He shifted his weight from side to side and finally grabbed her hand without turning around.

The elevator stopped. "Our floor," he said.

Sara didn't recognize his voice and barely avoided flashing the other men as she got off the elevator.

Simon held her arm tightly as he strode down a hallway much like the one they'd been in upstairs.

When he stopped abruptly in front of a door, Sara nearly barrelled into him. "Hold this." He thrust the plastic wrap at her. Still grasping her hand—like she was going anywhere—he fumbled with his keys.

"C'mon..." He swore.

Finally opening the door, he stopped just inside and stared at the burglar alarm, breathing heavily. "I can barely remember the code." He jabbed at a series of numbers, then hauled her inside and up against him, kicking the door shut with his foot.

He kissed her wildly, his hands roaming her body beneath her coat.

Grasping her hair at the nape, he pulled her head back. His eyes glittered. "You wanted fifteen seconds. Okay, you've got fifteen seconds to pick your spot. On the bed, on the floor or up against the wall. I don't care."

He released her and pushed the coat off her shoulders and onto the floor.

His gaze swept over her flushed body and then he shrugged out of his suit jacket and jerked at his tie. "I lied. You may not get fifteen seconds."

"Then I choose the bed."

"That way." He nodded to the doorway across the living room. "And, Sara?"

"Yes?"

"Run."

10

SHE MAY NOT HAVE RUN, but Sara did move very quickly and Simon was right behind her.

She reached the edge of the bed—a huge thing with cool, gray bedding—and turned around. "Simon?"

He gave her a look as he pulled his belt through the loops. A hot, focused look.

She was equally focused, but not so focused as to forget certain necessary rituals. "Have you got a condom, Simon? Or do you need to borrow some of my plastic wrap?"

He didn't crack a smile or stop looking at her. He did jerk open the nightstand drawer, reach inside and toss a generous handful next to the lamp.

"I do like the way you think."

He plucked one from the pile and ripped it open with his teeth.

In the same spirit, Sara ripped his shirt off his shoulders and that was as far as she got.

Simon hauled her to him and fused their mouths together. His hands covered her hips and he pressed them deliberately against him.

Twin groans mingled in their throats. Sara had spent

so long in a state of arousal, she'd thought Simon was never going to assuage all the throbbing and aching.

For long moments, they didn't move as Simon drove her mindless with drugging kisses.

Their desire for each other fed on itself, and far too quickly the kisses weren't enough. Sara wanted his hands on her and she wanted them on her now. "Touch me," she whispered, not at all sure he heard her, not at all sure she'd spoken the words aloud.

It didn't matter, because she felt his hand at her breast, and then his mouth. "Si—" The rest was lost as the air left her lungs and her knees threatened to collapse. They may have, but Simon held her so tightly against him she was in no danger of falling.

Falling onto the floor, that is. Falling into a vast pool where nothing existed but the sensations he was causing was a distinct possibility.

He raised his head and cupped her face in his hands. Their eyes locked for a potent moment, and then he urgently kissed her again, all the while backing her toward the bed.

She clutched at his shoulders as he scooped her up and threw her down on the bed.

Instantly, he was with her, pulling her hips close to his, settling between her legs. Sara started tearing at his shirt, but he made a sound, a growl, really, before he laced their fingers together and raised them above her head. Drawing back he gazed down at her, his eyes glazed with passion. She'd never seen that expression on a man's face before. It was primitive and elemental.

It was raw and it called to the very essence of her femaleness.

Simon entered her in one long, smooth thrust, filling her, claiming her.

She gasped softly because though she'd been ready, more than ready, it had been unexpected. Then again, it hadn't been. Not with him looking at her that way.

As he began to move, Simon closed his eyes and caught his lower lip between his teeth.

The explosion of heat surprised her, blasting her close to the edge. Not already...it wasn't possible. It had never happened this quickly....

But Simon, his head now buried in the pillow just above her, relentlessly increased the rhythm and Sara found she was already teetering on the precipice. She rocked her hips toward him, encouraging him to surge hard against her. When he slowed, she bit his shoulder.

He sucked the breath between his teeth and pounded her over the edge, shuddering his way after her.

She was falling and flying all at once, spiraling through the sky. Sara felt as though she'd swallowed fireworks—the whole grand finale on the Fourth of July. At the very least, she figured she'd burst a blood vessel.

And it went on and on, waves rippling through her, each one better than the last. She had to remind herself to breathe and when she did, she knew it had been a while as air rushed into her oxygen-starved lungs and she saw spots behind her eyelids.

She drew another huge breath, feeling wonderfully alive. She would never doubt Hayden's wisdom again. She would get Missy a used fur coat for a wedding gift. Or at least a lifetime supply of plastic wrap.

Simon hadn't moved and Sara enjoyed the weight of him pressing her back into bed. His breathing was still fast and hard, but slowing. She matched hers to his.

He'd been desperate for her, pure and simple. He'd been quiet on the surface, but oh, she'd been well rewarded for cracking that outward composure.

She rubbed his back, smiling as her fingers encountered cotton instead of skin.

"I'm sorry," he whispered next to her ear, then kissed it with exquisite tenderness.

So he hadn't taken off his shirt because he'd wanted her right then and there. How cool was that?

He unlaced their fingers and brushed her hair off her forehead. "Sara, I'm so, so very sorry."

Sorry? Sara turned her head as he dropped a kiss on her temple. "I'm not."

"I am." He kissed her cheek. "Very sorry." Her neck. "Sorry, sorry, sorry." A variety of other sensitive spots.

His face, when she could see it, was anguished.

"What are you sorry for?"

He grimaced. "I was no better than an animal."

"Oh, yeah." She closed her eyes at the memory she wouldn't ever forget.

"I was selfish and that was inexcusable. I can only say that I was just so damn desperate for you that I completely lost it." He sounded so guilty.

Another time, she might use that guilt, but not now. "Simon."

"I'd been thinking about you for days, and then there you were and you were naked and I...I'm so sorry." He nuzzled her neck, kissing the hollow beneath her jaw.

"You were provoked."

"No excuse."

"I enjoyed provoking you. Simon." She nudged his head up until he met her eyes. "Simon, never apologize for giving a woman the big 'O.'"

He blinked. "The big 'O'?"

Sara smiled and nodded. "One gigantic 'O,' followed by a couple of impressive 'O's,' a few medium 'O's,' then a whole bunch of little 'O's' just trailing after."

"You...'O'd'?"

"Oh, yeah. I cheery 'O'd' all over the place."

He searched her face, not sure if he could believe her. Something in her sated expression finally convinced him and he grinned with complete male satisfaction. It was great to see. "You'll forgive me for not noticing since I was dealing with my own big 'O.'"

"Yeah, I dealt with it, too. Hmm." She stretched beneath him. "You were outta control." And it was her turn to smile with satisfaction.

"You're pleased with yourself."

"Sure am." She traced her finger over his jaw until it found the little dimple in his chin. "I drove you wild."

"You drove me insane. I've been harboring this incredible desire for you—"

"Just say you had the hots for me."

"Red hots. Anyway, I do have somewhat more finesse at my disposal and I want the first time I make love to you to be special."

She sighed dreamily. "It was."

"That was sex. Primitive mating."

Sara could stand some more primitive mating. "So that's what I've been doing wrong. I've been settling for lukewarm lovemaking when I could have been having hot, primitive sex."

"When I make love to you, it'll be hot." He withdrew from her, then shifted until he sat up. "It'll be sizzling."

He spoke matter-of-factly, as though it was a given.

A shudder went through her. And she'd thought she was all o'd out. Sara propped herself on one elbow and pointed to his feet. "You seem very sure of yourself for someone who didn't even take off his shoes."

Simon pulled his shirt over his head without unbuttoning the only two buttons it had left, grinned and kicked off his shoes.

"And you seem very blasé for someone whose clothes are not only not in this apartment, but aren't even on this floor."

Sara's fingers flew to her mouth. "I'd forgotten about that."

Simon shucked off his pants. "Don't worry. You won't be needing them for a while."

"You know, just give me a roll of aluminum foil and I'm good to go."

He laughed, a full throated, throw-back-the-head laugh. Sara had never heard him do that before. He was relaxed. Confident. Sexy. And he was about to make love to her again.

Did it get any better than this?

Still chuckling, Simon unstrapped his watch and set it on the nightstand, then slipped out of his boxers.

Even naked, he looked elegant. He looked nude. Like an artist's nude. She just looked naked. But, hey. He didn't seem to mind.

"I was wondering when you'd get around to taking off those boxers. I've been naked in front of you for hours."

"A half hour, tops."

"Still, there's a significant exposure inequity, here."

He reached for the edge of the comforter and tugged it out from under her. "I'll make it up to you."

Sara slid under the sheets, high thread count sheets, she noticed.

When Simon tried to climb in after her, she stopped him. "Uh-uh. Stand up and turn around."

Giving her a quizzical look, he did so. She sighed a happy little sigh, thinking of all the paper jams Hayden had resorted to and then still had to imagine what he looked like. And now Sara knew, knew for all time. "Oh, thank you," she said fervently.

"Looking for a bruise?"

"I didn't pinch you hard enough to make a bruise. Besides, I rubbed it all better. No, I was just admiring the view."

IT PLEASED SIMON to know that Sara found him attractive and wasn't afraid to show it. He turned and got into bed with her. "I've got a pretty good view, too." He ran a hand from her shoulder to her calf. Her skin was warm and soft and still flushed from the sex and possibly the coat.

She'd completely blown his mind. And no matter how many O's she claimed, he, well, "O'd" her. He wanted to see her surrender, see her face when she was completely caught up in passion.

He wanted to savor the way she tasted, explore the texture of her skin and hear the sounds she made when she didn't know she was making them.

He wanted to find her hidden freckles, learn about the tiny scar on her hip, and discover the secret places that made her writhe.

He wanted to watch her sleep. He wanted to wake up next to her and discover whether she was a morning person or adorably grumpy. He wanted to love her awake and bring her coffee in bed.

He wanted her in his life, now and always.

This woman was his.

Simon drew a shuddering breath.

"What is it?" Sara asked.

It was too soon—for her, not for him. But the longer Simon looked at her, lying all tousled in his bed, her lips reddened from his kisses, the more the words struggled to burst free.

"It's jet lag, isn't it?" She sat up, unselfconsciously letting the sheet fall to her waist. "You must be exhausted, and, well," she looked down with false modesty, "drained."

He cupped her cheek. "I have to tell you something before..."

"What?" She drew the sheet up, her voice filled with instant wariness.

He smoothed his thumb against her cheek. "I'm going to make love to you...because I'm *in* love with you."

Her lips parted and her eyes went soft. "Simon..."

"Shh." He placed a finger on her lips. "I know it's too soon, but I wanted you to know."

Sara blinked back tears.

"I didn't want you to cry!"

She waved her hand and sniffed. "I fell in love with you when you didn't ask about the coat."

The coat? Just a few minutes ago? "Not until then? I've loved you almost from the beginning."

"But I didn't want to fall in love with you!" she wailed.

He was floored. "Why not?"

"I didn't want to get hurt. I know you have responsibilities with Kayla and her mother and..." She trailed off.

"What?"

"I don't think I can handle them always coming first."

"They won't," he assured her.

"They have so far," Sara said quietly. "You drop whatever you're doing, interrupt any conversation—any kiss—and instantly give them your complete attention."

He remembered that interrupted kiss. "Kayla hasn't developed a lot of social skills yet."

Sara gave him a direct look. "Joanna has."

Yes, Joanna. "I realize it seems as though Joanna is manipulating me, but I'm aware of what she's doing."

"Then why do you let her do it?"

He exhaled. "It's easier and...I don't want to tick her off to the point that she doesn't let me see Kayla anymore."

"Oh, Simon." Sara looked stricken. "That's emotional blackmail."

"I can put up with it for a few years. The thing is, Kayla needs me, needs a stabilizing male influence and I'd rather be an active part of her life than leave it to some stranger when Joanna starts dating again. She doesn't date yet, you know."

"Why would she? She wants you."

Sara couldn't be serious. "No way."

"You sure?"

They stared at each other.

Simon considered Joanna. Though he didn't often think of it, he could remember their college days and the way Joanna behaved toward him then was completely different from the way she did now. "College was another lifetime ago. We're not even the same people. Trust me, now we're only tolerating one another."

He tugged at the sheet she still clutched to herself. "Besides, I'm in love with you." He took Sara in his arms and rocked her gently back and forth. "I'll never purposely hurt you but I'm not perfect. There are bound to be bumps in the road."

"I know."

There was silence and he enjoyed the feel of her in his arms.

And then she chuckled. "Why look. There's a bump right now. And a pretty impressive bump it is, too."

As he kissed her back into the pillows, Simon wished all bumps could be smoothed so enjoyably. He was convinced that all Sara needed was reassurance, which he was more than happy to provide.

First, he reassured her mouth, then her cheeks, then her earlobes and the curve of her neck. Her breasts needed lots of reassuring.

"Simon!" She shuddered his name, so he kissed his way to the crook of her elbow.

She twisted toward him. "What are you doing?"

"Kissing your elbow. You have nice elbows."

She opened her eyes and looked at him in exasperation.

"Relax. Enjoy. I'm making love to you and I intend to take my time."

"Well, my elbows are feeling plenty loved, I can tell you."

He chuckled and skimmed his hand over her abdomen to the curve of her waist. His fingers stroked the skin at the top of her hip. "How about your back? Does your back feel loved?"

"My back is just fine. It wouldn't know what to do with the attention." She tried to move his hand, but he wouldn't let her.

"Sara—has a man ever made love to your back?"

She gave him a startled look. "Why would he do that?"

Simon moved closer and draped his hand lower, low enough to draw lazy circles in the small of her back. He smiled. "Roll over and I'll show you."

A RINGING PHONE dragged Simon from a dreamless slumber. Every muscle ached. Some in a jet lag way, but some in a sex-after-a-long-dry-spell way. He looked down at Sara curled up next to him and felt such a wave of feeling the intensity made his hands shake as he leaned over the bed and searched his pants pocket for his cell phone.

He answered it, stepping away from the bed so he wouldn't wake her.

"Hello?" What time was it?

"Simon? Where are you?"

Joanna. "Home. I fell asleep." He rubbed at his face.

"Well, the girls were starving. I had to go ahead and feed them."

Right. He'd mentioned possibly having dinner with Kayla. He shouldn't have answered his cell phone on the drive home from the airport. Kayla would never have known he was back in the country. "It's good they've eaten." Presumably the other girl was Amber. "When Kayla mentioned it, I told her I'd get back to her."

"And you didn't."

"I fell asleep." He really resented the tone in Joanna's voice. "When I talked to her, I hadn't even been home yet. There was nothing definite planned."

"Kayla is a child. You can't expect her to understand when you say you'll get back to her and then you don't. You should have seen her sitting here waiting. It nearly broke my heart."

Somehow, he couldn't picture Kayla hanging around a phone. "Joanna, I'm tired. Apologize to Kayla for me and I'll talk with her tomorrow."

"Just a minute—she's all packed and ready for you to come get her. She's spending the weekend with you. And we didn't think you'd mind if Amber came, too. Her parents are out of town."

"Of course I mind!"

"Why? Amber is the sweetest thing. She's no trouble—"

"I'm not talking about Amber. I do not remember inviting Kayla to spend the weekend with me. I was still going to be in Glasgow, remember?"

"This is the weekend of Callie's wedding in Santa Fe. You *do* remember that."

Simon closed his eyes. He did. "Yes, but since when does a weekend begin on Thursday?"

"My flight leaves tomorrow while they're at school. So it's a good thing you *are* back, because I was having a terrible time finding a weekend sitter."

"Joanna..."

"When shall I tell them to expect you? Or shall I bring them to you? We're ready to leave any time."

"It's late and I'm tired. Let them sleep over there tonight."

"That would not be good for Kayla."

"It's her home. How can it not be good?"

"You know how important it is to her self-esteem to know that she's loved. I don't know how she'll handle the disappointment." He'd dealt with a disappointed Kayla's tantrums before.

Simon tried to think his way out of this, but his mind was too sluggish. He turned back around and found Sara sitting up, her knees drawn to her chest. She was looking at him in the dim light.

Damn it. "I'll be there in forty-five minutes."

Sara rested her head on her knees.

Simon hung up and walked over to the bed. "Sara, I'm sorry. Kayla spending this weekend with me was planned a month ago."

"It's okay." She gave him a smile that didn't fool him for a minute. "I'll leave as soon as you get me my clothes—or that aluminum foil."

"Sara, I don't want you to go. Not like this."

"I'm not planning to leave like this. I'm planning to wear clothes. Preferably my own. Unfortunately, I'll need your help since my purse and the key to Mrs. Galloway's apartment are locked inside together.''

The connection that had been forged between them, the one he'd thought nothing could break, was gone. "Stay. I'm calling Joanna—''

"No. She'd want an explanation and...it's just better that I go.''

Afterward, when Sara had dressed and he'd walked with her down to the parking garage, he said, "I'll call you later after they're asleep.''

She shook her head. "Don't bother.''

"I know you're angry, Sara, but try to understand.''

"I do understand. And I'm not angry. I'm realistic.'' She gave him a quick kiss. "Enjoy the slumber party with your sister.''

HAYDEN AND MISSY didn't even wait until lunch the next day. They appeared at the door of Sara's cubicle at eight-thirty in the morning.

"Thank God you're all right! You scared me. I would have called 9-1-1 if I'd known where you were.''

"I'm sorry, Hayden.'' Sara felt guilty for ignoring her answering machine. She'd been afraid she'd find a call from Simon when she got home.

"Well, what happened? Who was at the door?''

"Simon.''

They gasped.

Sara sighed. "The fur coat Saran Wrap thing?'' She made an okay sign. "Very effective.''

"You and Simon?'' Missy's eyes widened.

Sara allowed herself to remember a few of the more pleasant memories. There were so many from which to choose. "Oh, yeah."

"Well?" Hayden asked as Sara had known she would.

Sara closed her eyes. "Rolls-Royce all the way." Until it plowed into a wall of Joanna's making. Tears burned her eyes. "The thing is, I don't think I can do that with another man."

"It? You mean sex?"

"Sex in no way describes what we did."

"Oh, puhleeze," Hayden scoffed. "New lovers always think they're the only ones...yadda yadda yadda."

"But why would you want to sleep with another man?" Missy asked. "Isn't Simon the one?"

A tear leaked out. Hayden grabbed a tissue from the box next to Sara's computer and handed it to her.

"He's the one. But he's not the right one. He came back early from the trip just to see me and we were asleep in his apartment when Joanna called."

Missy glowered. "That witch."

"Don't flatter her," Hayden said.

"And the next thing I knew, Kayla and her friend, Amber, were coming over to spend the weekend."

Hayden winced and pressed her forehead with her fingers. "Let me clarify—you're in his bed and he throws you out for his *sister?*"

Sara nodded. "He didn't throw me out, but it was clear that I'd have to leave."

"Well, you couldn't really stay there and sleep with him...I mean, she is only twelve," Missy said.

"I know," Sara said. "And it'll happen again and again. I thought I could take it, but I can't."

"That man is not right in the head," was all Hayden had to say.

"Okay. Enough." Sara sniffed and wiped her eyes. "So this one stings a little—a lot. I'll just keep looking. It's actually good that I won't feel anything for anybody for a while because then I can make smart, logical choices before romantic feelings muddy the waters."

Hayden and Missy looked at each other.

"I want to get right back in the saddle," Sara told them. "I have two names from the Barre Belles, and anybody else you two have found. See what you can set up for me. I'm free all next week."

After they left, Sara went through a couple more tissues, grateful that she'd put on waterproof mascara that morning. The truth was, she felt used, even though she'd been an enthusiastic participant. Still, no matter how attractive, no matter how good a lover Simon had proved to be—who knew about backs?—he wasn't the one for her. She wanted to be first in a man's life and Simon clearly had other priorities.

He didn't call her, but when she got back from lunch, a single red rose lay across her computer keyboard.

11

It was Friday night and Hayden tried to get Sara to go bar hopping, but Sara was still feeling too down.

She got home, got into her fluffy robe—the one Hayden had wanted her to replace with a silk one—and popped her *Pride and Prejudice* DVD into the machine. She didn't feel like eating, but had two flavors of ice cream on standby, just in case.

She turned the air conditioner to frigid, settled onto her couch with its new soft pillows and wrapped herself in the chenille throw. Oh, yeah. And put a box of tissues on the coffee table.

At nine-thirty, the phone rang. She didn't answer it.

At nine-forty, the phone rang. She didn't answer it. At nine-forty-two, the phone rang. She glared at it. At nine-forty-three, her cell phone rang, so she dug it out of her purse.

"Sara?" Hayden shouted in her ear, loud music playing in the background.

"What?" Sara shouted back.

"Answer your phone. Simon wants to talk to you."

"I don't want to talk to him."

"He needs your help."

"I'm no longer providing that kind of help."

"Sara, the guy sounds desperate. Talk to him. He left his number on your machine."

Fine. She couldn't have him bothering her friends.

His was the first message. "Sara…I need your help. Something is going on with the girls and they won't tell me what. Amber's locked herself in the bathroom and won't come out. I'm out of my element here. Joanna's not answering her cell and Amber's parents are out of town. If you get this message, please call. It doesn't matter what time."

The second one was from Simon. "Sara, here's my number in case you don't have it." He left it, then, "I don't suppose you're there? Please pick up if you are."

The next message was Hayden, telling her that Simon was looking for her.

Sighing, Sara called him.

"Sara!" The relief in his voice was palpable.

"What's going on?"

"Amber won't come out of the bathroom and Kayla gets nearly hysterical when I ask her why."

Let's see…twelve-year-old girls…bathroom…won't talk to big brother… "I think I've got it. Let me talk to Kayla."

She could hear Simon coaxing Kayla to come to the phone.

"Sara?"

"Hi, Kayla. Did Amber start her period?"

"Yes!"

"First time?"

"Yes." She sounded scared.

"Hey, it's okay. I'm coming over there and I'll bring supplies. Don't worry. There's nothing to be scared of. This is natural and we need to celebrate. Put Simon back on."

"Don't tell him!"

"I won't." Seconds later, she was talking to Simon. "Okay, here's what you need to do."

"Is she sick?"

"No. Your job is to go to the video store and get movies that girls their age would like to see—make sure one is *Princess Bride*. Ask the guys there. Then, go to the store for chocolate and vanilla ice cream and sundae sauces—hot fudge and caramel, and maybe strawberry. Get whipped cream in a can, too. Not the fake stuff, the real thing. Got it?"

There was a silence. "Anything else?" he asked wryly.

"Maybe pizza."

"We can order that."

"Okay."

"And then what do I do? Use a hot fudge sundae to lure Amber out of the bathroom?"

"No. I'm coming over there. I'll take care of Amber. You go shopping and don't ask questions."

"Got it."

"Take your time."

Simon was gone when Sara got over there with an assortment of feminine supplies. A man who could follow directions. She liked that.

Once Amber had calmed down and been taken care

of, Sara had a long talk with both girls, and was grati-
fied to learn that they knew the birds-and-bees basics.
Still, she figured some reinforcement couldn't hurt.

By the time Simon got back, they'd had a great female bonding session and Sara was enjoying her role
as the wise woman immensely. It wasn't often that she
felt wise. Especially when she saw Simon. He sent such
a scorching gaze across the brown paper grocery sacks
he carried, Sara was surprised they didn't catch fire.

"What movies did you get?"

Simon handed Kayla a bag of at least a dozen movies
and perceptively didn't say anything to Amber. The
girls took the bag into the living room next to the TV.

"Thanks for coming." Simon reached for her. Sara
planned to resist, but found herself kissing him instead.

Not good.

"I've missed you," Simon whispered.

Sara sighed against him, but didn't say anything.

"Will you stay?"

Keep it light. She pushed herself out of his arms. "I
don't know." She peered into the grocery sacks. "It depends on what toppings you got."

He flashed her a grin and started bringing jars out of
the sack. "Looks like you're staying. I've got pineap-
ple—"

"*What?* Ick."

"Hot fudge."

"Now you're talking."

"Butterscotch."

"Eh."

"Caramel."

"Better."

"Strawberry."

"Okay."

"Marshmallow."

"Uh..."

"Mini M&M's."

"Wow. Didn't think of those." Sara took the jar from him, opened it, and ate a few.

"Chopped peanuts."

"What did you do—buy one of everything?"

"Except the regular chocolate flavor. Couldn't see the point with the hot fudge."

"Good thinking." She closed the jar of mini M&M's and set it on the counter. "You're a great big brother, you know that?"

"You haven't even seen the ice cream, yet." He brought out chocolate and vanilla, two cans of whipped cream and a jar of maraschino cherries.

Sara made a face. "I hate those things."

"Then *you* don't have to eat them." Simon opened the jar and popped one in his mouth.

"Can you tie the stem into a knot with your tongue?"

"I don't know." He tried, making her laugh with his faces.

If his sister and her friend hadn't been in the next room, Sara would have grabbed Simon and a can of whipped cream and headed for the bedroom.

But the girls were there, serving to remind Sara why

staying with Simon would only lead to frustration and hurt.

"Do I get to know what this is all about?" Simon asked.

"No," Sara said. "I will, however, tell you that Amber is a woman now."

It took him a minute. "Oh. Oh!" A look of panic crossed his face.

"Relax and play dumb. It's all taken care of."

He got out bowls and spoons. "Is, uh, is Kayla a woman yet?"

"Not yet."

"Good." He looked at her. "I think."

"Don't think. Open the ice cream."

Kayla and Amber were thrilled with the sundaes. Simon had big guy-sized bowls and let them make huge gooey creations that gave them all queasy stomachs.

They watched a movie—even Simon, who contentedly sat through a movie geared to preteen girls, with Sara on the sofa next to him.

Did he have to be such a great guy?

If he weren't a great guy, he wouldn't be paying attention to his sister and you wouldn't like him very much.

Well, yes, there was that.

SARA WAS the perfect woman for him. He looked at her sitting next to him on the sofa, her head leaning on his arm and felt a surge of emotion. He wanted her there every night.

He wanted her in his bed every night.

He'd been wrong about the connection between them being lost. It was still there, it just needed polishing.

It amazed him that Kayla got along so well with Sara—truthfully better than with her own mother. If Kayla mouthed off, Sara called her on it—once poking Kayla with her foot.

And Kayla responded by laughing, but cheerfully behaving once more. Simon didn't intend to start kicking Kayla, but he realized he might be too serious around her.

The girl had lost her father—his father—and he'd been letting her get away with obnoxious behavior because of it. Joanna, too.

He tried to imagine Joanna sitting here and felt nothing but unenthusiasm.

The movie ended and they turned it off.

"Okay, bedtime," Sara told the girls. Simon thought it was an excellent idea. "You two rinse your dishes and put them in the dishwasher."

"I don't want to go to bed," Kayla pouted.

Not this again. Simon geared up for a protracted whining session.

"I didn't say you had to go to sleep," Sara said. "Just get in bed."

Kayla looked uncertain.

"Move it." Sara took Simon's dish and walked toward the kitchen.

Without another word or whine or protest, Amber and Kayla followed her.

How did she do that?

After the girls were in bed, giggling behind the closed door, Sara picked up her purse. "I'd better be—"

"We need to talk," he said.

"Wow." She let her purse strap slide down her arm. "That's my line."

"But you aren't saying it."

"No." She gave him a challenging look.

Simon went for the big guns. "I love you."

"Yeah."

He noticed that she didn't say it back. Well, she'd said it back last night. "I want to be with you."

"*Be* with me?"

"I want you in my life."

She ran her hand through her hair. "Your life is crowded, Simon."

"You mean Kayla."

"I mean Kayla and Joanna."

"Joanna is Kayla's mother. I can't avoid her. As for Kayla, I'm her brother. I do have certain responsibilities toward her." He'd thought Sara had understood that.

"That's right—brother. You're her brother. Not father. But Joanna has manipulated you into acting like Kayla's father and it confuses her."

"And you know all this from being around her for a few hours."

Sara's lips twisted wryly. "It didn't take that long."

"You're jealous of a twelve-year-old."

She sighed heavily. "I knew you would say that eventually, which is why I didn't want to have this conversation with you." She turned away, then back. "I'm not going to make you think you have to choose between me and your sister. That's not what this is about. Of course you should be a part of your sister's life. I don't expect you to spend every minute with me."

"Then what's the problem?"

"I'm looking for somebody who will put me first in a relationship. And you won't do that."

"You *are* making me choose between you."

She shook her head. "What I'd like for you to do is take a good long look at the way things are. After the baseball game, you had to leave the very next day because Joanna caught us kissing."

"No. It was because Kayla was hesitant about summer camp."

"That is her mother's problem!"

"It's my problem, too."

She exhaled forcefully and held out her hands as though calming herself. "Nevertheless, it was interesting timing, don't you think?"

"Unfortunate timing. I wanted to be with you. You have to know that."

"But I didn't!"

He should have called her. Simon tried to hold her,

but Sara stepped away from him and his arms dropped to his sides.

"Sara, last night was one of the highlights of my life." He looked for and saw a brief softening in her expression, but she turned away.

"Last night, you were supposed to be in Glasgow."

That again. "I told you, this weekend had been planned—"

"Simon!" Sara made a frustrated sound. "What would Joanna have done if you were still in Glasgow? Do you honestly think she hadn't made alternative childcare arrangements? Do you think she was just going to leave Kayla by herself? And why did Kayla *and* Amber have to come right then and there? I heard you tell Joanna you were tired. You could have picked the girls up from school the next day. Didn't you anyway?"

"But I'd talked to Kayla already. She knew I was back."

"So?"

"Kayla needs stability," he said slowly. "I didn't want her to think I was rejecting her or abandoning her."

"By making her wait one day?" She scoffed. "I'll tell you who felt rejected and abandoned—me! We were in bed together—sleeping. After being in bed together not sleeping. You told me you loved me!"

"I do!"

Sara shook her head. "I'll tell you what went on. Joanna wanted to keep us apart. She suspected we were together. It's nothing personal against me. She'll try to break up any relationship of yours because it will keep you from spending all your time raising *her* daughter.''

Simon had been sympathetic and understanding up until that point, but Sara clearly couldn't see his position. ''I think you've gone too far.''

''Actually, I haven't gone far enough. You and Joanna act like a divorced couple with joint custody. She's playing on your guilt for forgetting about Kayla when she was a baby. And I've got to hand it to her, she's good because from what you told me, she should be the one who feels guilty.''

''But I should have acknowledged Kayla.''

''You were human and you were hurt. Don't let her play you.''

''So every time Joanna or Kayla calls, I'm supposed to say, 'Sorry. I'll have to get Sara's permission to talk to you'?''

''No, but you have to put us, that's me and you and our relationship, first. That is, if you want one.''

He stared at her, but she wouldn't back down. She seemed so sure of herself and she was being so unreasonable. ''So, I do have to choose between you, except that I'm always supposed to choose you.''

She looked at him for a long moment. ''Yeah.''

There it was. Last night's incident would be replayed over and over again until Kayla was old enough to take care of herself. "Sara, I can't be what you want me to be right now."

"I know." She picked up her purse. "That's why I can't be with you."

"SIMON LOOKS LIKE HELL." Hayden was late to lunch. "And you don't look much better."

"Thanks a lot."

Missy dug in her bag. "Here, Sara, borrow some of my concealer stick. I'm trying several different shades for my wedding."

"Hush," Hayden said to Missy. "Don't say the word 'wedding' around her."

"It's okay." Sara smiled brightly. "I'm fine. I had my ride in the Rolls and there are a lot of women who never get that much. I'm over it. Over him."

Missy and Hayden looked pointedly at Sara's lunch, which consisted of two pieces of coconut cream pie.

"I didn't have breakfast," Sara explained.

Hayden studied her. "You're still in love with Simon."

"Yes." She filled her mouth with meringue from one piece, which she was eating in layers. The other piece, she was eating the three layers at once. A person could use the variety.

"Yet you won't fight for him," Missy said.

"No." Sara ate a three-layered forkful. "Can't win."

"I think you could take Joanna on," Hayden said.

Sara dropped her fork and drilled Hayden with a look. "I was in his bed after two sessions of mind-blowing sex *and* he'd said the 'L' word. And she calls, *wakes him up*, and he goes running. She didn't even have to drive her daughter over to him. Oh, no. He gets rid of me and goes and gets her." She picked up her fork. "*That* is a no-win situation. Then I have to explain why it's a no-win situation to him and of course he doesn't believe me and gets ticked off besides. So, he's out of the picture. Hook me up with new candidates, please." She dug into the coconut cream layer.

"Simon Northrup never struck me as a stupid man," Hayden mused. "Latent case of testosterone poisoning, I guess." She sighed. "Whatcha got for her, Missy?"

"More Barre Belles' connections. They both check out. One's thirty-one, and the other is twenty-eight and divorced, no children. Presentable looks, both solvent."

"Sounds fine," Sara said. "Either one."

"I'll make some calls," Missy offered.

"I have a tentative meeting with a lawyer who's bringing a friend with him tonight," Hayden told her.

Sara had made her way down to the crust. "Fabulous. Let's go. I'm ready."

IT WAS AN ODD THING, but now that Sara wasn't emotionally needy, she was attracting men as she never had before. The lawyer was breathtakingly handsome—or would have seemed so if she hadn't already seen Simon. He asked for her number and actually called her. So did Hayden's date, but Sara pretended she never got that message.

Then she went out with both Barre Belles' connections—incredibly nice guys. And *they* both called her. Go figure.

She fed their stats to Missy, who inputted them into Sara's spreadsheet.

Hayden found out that her lawyer date had called Sara and insisted that she was finished with him, so, because she'd been on a nice-guy roll, Sara went out with him, too.

And her nice guy streak ended.

It was a work night and after drinks and dinner, Sara was ready to go home. Make no mistake, he was charming and generous and good-looking, but he was no Simon.

Simon had poisoned her for all other men.

"Where are we going?" she asked when her date missed the exit off the freeway to her apartment.

"My place," he said.

She looked at him, looked at his mouth, tried to imagine kissing that mouth...and couldn't do it. "Look, I've had a nice time, but I've got to go to work tomorrow."

"It's not that late. I'm not ready for the evening to end." He smiled, reached over and put his hand on her thigh, his fingers searching beneath the hem of her skirt.

Not this. She had no patience or desire for this. She removed his hand. "I want to go home."

"My place is nicer."

He hadn't even seen her place. "I meant home alone."

"Fine." He whipped the car to the side of the road so quickly, her head jerked painfully to the side.

Reaching across her, he opened the door. "You want to go home, so go."

"Oh, come on. You're not some frustrated teenager and I didn't order the lobster."

"It's worse. You wasted my time."

She would have snapped at him to bill her at his going rate, but he probably would have. "You aren't going to take me home?"

"Be happy to take you home later."

Sara looked around. It was after dark, but this was a nice residential area. "I'll take my chances now."

"Just remember that it was your choice."

He was probably legally covering himself. "Jerk." She got out, not bothering to shut the door.

He leaned over, slammed it and within moments, roared off.

She honestly thought she'd see red taillights as he came to his senses and backed up to get her. They disappeared around the bend and she stared into the darkness for several minutes before realizing that she'd actually been dumped by the side of the road.

Sara pulled her cell phone out of her purse. What did women do before cell phones? She called Hayden. No answer. She called Missy. No answer. She tried Hayden's cell, but it went over to her voice mail.

Great. What was the use of having a cell phone if nobody answered? She looked around. She was on a winding two-lane street with houses set way back from the sidewalks. The trees made it dark, but it would probably be safe to approach one of the homes and ask someone to call a cab.

Or she could call Simon. Honestly, as many times as he'd come to her rescue, she almost expected him to come driving up. But he was busy with Kayla, no doubt.

She called him anyway.

"Sara! Hi." His voice warmed. "I'm glad you called."

"You might not be." She heard music in the background. Kayla-type music. "I—is Kayla over there?"

He hesitated before answering. "Yes. Joanna's got finals and Kayla is staying over here so she can study."

Sara rolled her eyes. "Okay. So you're busy—"

"What's up?"

Sara drew a breath. "I couldn't reach Hayden or Missy. My date abandoned me in the wilds of Memorial. I need a white knight."

"What do you mean 'abandoned you'?" He sounded outraged.

Good. She was outraged, too. "I mean he wanted to go back to his place, I didn't, and so he let me out of the car."

"By the side of the road?"

"Yes."

"Where are you?"

"I'm not exactly sure. We got off the freeway and didn't drive too far. I'll walk to a cross street and let you know."

"Stay put. I'll find you."

She was surprised and, yes, glad to have an excuse to see Simon again. This dating thing wasn't working and it wasn't just because of her experience tonight. She'd met several really nice men whose only problem was that they weren't Simon.

Despite his instructions, Sara walked until she got to a cross street and called him. Less than five minutes later, he pulled up beside her.

"Just how fast did you drive?" she asked as she got in.

"Fast," came a voice from the back seat. Kayla. "Now hurry up and take her home. I'm missing my show!"

Simon glanced back at her in the rearview mirror. "So, you're missing your show. Get over it."

"You used to be a lot nicer." Kayla slumped down in the seat.

"You didn't," Simon said and Sara stared at him.

What had happened to those two?

"Are you still going to make me finish my homework even though I didn't get to watch my show?"

"You bet. That's what your mom told me to do."

"Man!"

Something had changed in their relationship. They sounded like squabbling...siblings. They sounded like brother and sister. Sara felt hope beating its poor bruised wings against her rib cage.

"Hey." She turned in the seat so she could see Kayla.

"What happened to sisterly solidarity? I was abandoned by a creep."

"You shouldn't go out with creeps. You should go out with my brother."

"Hear that?" Simon asked. "She doesn't think I'm a creep."

"You're only a creep when it comes to homework and talking on the phone."

Sara looked at Simon. "Really? Talking on the phone?"

"A little punk called her."

"Cory isn't a punk! Simon took away my cell phone."

"I told you, no phone until your homework gets done."

"Cory had a question about the homework! That's why he called me on your phone. And then Simon listened in!"

"They weren't talking about homework."

"That's an invasion of privacy! Don't you think that's horrible, Sara?"

Sara smiled at Simon. They were at a stoplight, so he looked over at her. Their eyes met and understanding passed between them.

"I think it's wonderful," Sara said.

LATER THAT NIGHT, Simon stopped by her apartment after dropping Kayla back home. "I know it's late," he began.

"Fortunately, not too late." Sara smiled and led him

over to the couch with the soft cushions and the chenille throw. She'd lit candles, put a jazzy-bluesy CD on
the stereo, and brewed two cups of herbal tea, which
she'd placed on a woven mat atop the coffee table.

She was wearing a long, silk wrap robe, under which
she was wearing exactly nothing. If the conversation
went well, she'd let him know.

"Thanks for letting me come over."

"Thanks for rescuing me once again."

He sat on the sofa an arm's length away, but his gaze
was as intense as ever. It roamed over her. "Are you
wearing anything under that?"

She smiled. "I'll tell you after we talk."

"If you're not wearing anything under that, we
won't have to talk."

"If we don't talk, you'll never find out."

"Choose your topic."

She drew her feet toward her. "You and Kayla. You
acted different tonight."

"I had a very long, painfully blunt conversation with
Joanna. You probably won't be surprised to find out
that you were right about nearly everything."

"What wasn't I right about?"

"Okay, you were right about everything."

"That's more like it." Sara rewarded him by reaching for her tea, knowing that the neckline of her robe
would gape a little bit.

"I had no idea that Joanna thought it was possible..." He trailed off with a shake of his head.

Sara had absolutely no trouble filling in the rest of

the sentence. Joanna had some nerve trying to get Simon back.

"We're in family counseling," he said.

"Why didn't you tell me?"

"Didn't know if it would work. We started out with daily sessions the first week. Now we're at three times a week." He smiled the sweetest smile at her. "I'm learning how to be a big brother."

"I'm glad."

He inched closer to her. "You really aren't wearing anything under that robe, are you?"

Sara merely sipped her tea.

"I wasn't fair to you before."

"I know."

"I can't believe how screwed up things were." He glanced at her. "How about a little hint?"

Sara pulled the hem of the robe up to her knees.

"Sara—can we start again?"

"Start what again?"

"You aren't making this easy for me."

"I need to hear a certain amount of groveling to repair the damage to my self-esteem." As she spoke, the robe slipped off her shoulder.

Simon swallowed, his eyes on her shoulder. "I was an idiot?"

The robe slipped off her other shoulder.

"I was a well-meaning, but deluded fool?"

"That's pretty good," she said.

"They why didn't more of your robe slip off?"

Sara looked into the distance. "I'm just lacking a definitive something…"

His cell phone rang.

Sara raised her eyebrow.

He let it ring again. "Am I allowed to answer the phone?"

She shrugged a bare shoulder.

"I should have turned it off." He checked the number on the display, then gave Sara an apologetic look. "The next time I'll turn it off, I swear. Hello? Kayla? I'm..."

Sara saw the struggle on his face, then his resolve. "I'll have to fix your computer some other time. I'm busy."

He listened some more. "I suggest you call the punk for math help. I'm busy now." He frowned. "I can't talk with your mother right now. I'm busy and I'm hanging up the phone. She can call a repairman. That's what they do. Repair things."

"Simon!" Sara heard Kayla's voice over the phone.

He closed his eyes. Then they opened as understanding crossed his face. He raised his eyebrow. "Kayla says to tell you good-night." He punched off the phone. "That was a test, wasn't it?"

Sara smiled. Kayla had played her part frighteningly well. "Can you blame me?"

"I guess not." He leaned toward her and ran a finger along the line of her bare shoulders. "So, did I pass?"

Sara lay back on the sofa and let the robe slither open. "You passed. Want to try for bonus points?"

MANY BONUS POINTS LATER, in the darkness of Sara's room, on her bed with the six hundred thread count sheets, Simon nuzzled her ear and asked sleepily, "Will you marry me?"

Sara drew in a long breath. "Ask me again when we aren't in bed."

Immediately, Simon sat up, swung his legs over the side and pulled Sara out of bed.

"What are you doing?" she protested.

"Pulling you out of bed to ask you to marry me. I think you might say yes."

Her heart started hammering. "Simon—"

"That's not yes. I know what you're going to say. You're going to say that it's too soon, but Sara, we're perfect for each other. Even our faults are compatible."

It would never get better than this and she knew it. "Yes."

He stared at her. "Yes, our faults are compatible, or yes, you'll marry me?"

"I have no faults. Yes, I'll marry you."

He laughed and swung her against him so hard the air left her lungs. But it might have anyway. There wasn't enough room for both air and that much happiness.

Simon set her down. "One more thing—will you wear a fur coat if I buy you one?"

She'd wear fur anything. "Make it a fake."

"As long as you know my love is real."

"Then I'll wear it." Sara grinned. "Only for you."

Simon angled his head for a kiss. "Perfect."

* * * * *

HARLEQUIN®
Temptation®

Coming to a bookstore near you...

**The True Blue Calhouns trilogy
by bestselling author Julie Kistler**

Meet Jake, a cop who plays by the rules in

#957 HOT PROSPECT
(January 2004)

Deal with Sean, rebel and police detective in

#961 CUT TO THE CHASE
(February 2004)

Fall for Coop, rookie with a yen for danger in

#965 PACKING HEAT
(March 2004)

Three sinfully sexy very arresting men...
Ladies, watch out!

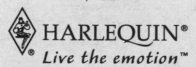

HARLEQUIN®
Live the emotion™

Visit us at www.canwetemptyou.com

HTTBR

Stories of shocking truths revealed!

PRIVATE SCANDALS

A brand-new collection from

JOANNA WAYNE
JUDY CHRISTENBERRY
TORI CARRINGTON

From three of the romance genre's most enthralling authors
comes this trio of novellas about secret agendas, deep passions
and hidden pasts. But not all scandals can be kept private!

Coming in January 2004.

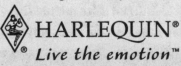

HARLEQUIN®
Live the emotion™

Visit us at www.eHarlequin.com

PHPS

If you enjoyed what you just read,
then we've got an offer you can't resist!

Take 2 bestselling love stories FREE!

Plus get a FREE surprise gift!

Clip this page and mail it to Harlequin Reader Service®

IN U.S.A.
3010 Walden Ave.
P.O. Box 1867
Buffalo, N.Y. 14240-1867

IN CANADA
P.O. Box 609
Fort Erie, Ontario
L2A 5X3

YES! Please send me 2 free Harlequin Temptation® novels and my free surprise gift. After receiving them, if I don't wish to receive anymore, I can return the shipping statement marked cancel. If I don't cancel, I will receive 4 brand-new novels each month, before they're available in stores. In the U.S.A., bill me at the bargain price of $3.57 plus 25¢ shipping and handling per book and applicable sales tax, if any*. In Canada, bill me at the bargain price of $4.24 plus 25¢ shipping and handling per book and applicable taxes**. That's the complete price and a savings of 10% off the cover prices—what a great deal! I understand that accepting the 2 free books and gift places me under no obligation ever to buy any books. I can always return a shipment and cancel at any time. Even if I never buy another book from Harlequin, the 2 free books and gift are mine to keep forever.

142 HDN DNT5
342 HDN DNT6

Name	(PLEASE PRINT)	
Address	Apt.#	
City	State/Prov.	Zip/Postal Code

* Terms and prices subject to change without notice. Sales tax applicable in N.Y.
** Canadian residents will be charged applicable provincial taxes and GST.
All orders subject to approval. Offer limited to one per household and not valid to current Harlequin Temptation® subscribers.
® are registered trademarks of Harlequin Enterprises Limited.

TEMP02   ©1998 Harlequin Enterprises Limited

e◆HARLEQUIN.com

Looking for today's most popular
books at great prices?
At www.eHarlequin.com, we offer:

- An **extensive selection** of romance
  books by top authors!

- **New** releases, Themed Collections
  and hard-to-find **backlist.**

- A sneak peek at Upcoming books.

- Enticing book **excerpts** and **back
  cover copy!**

- Read recommendations from other
  readers (and post your own)!

- Find out what everybody's reading
  in **Bestsellers.**

- **Save BIG** with everyday discounts
  and exclusive online offers!

- Easy, convenient **24-hour shopping.**

- Our **Romance Legend** will help select
  reading that's *exactly* right for you!

**Your purchases are 100%
guaranteed—so shop online
at www.eHarlequin.com today!**

INTBB1

**If you're a fan of sensual romance
you *simply* must read…**

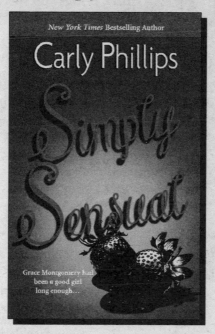

The third sizzling title in Carly Phillips's *Simply* trilogy.

"4 STARS—Sizzle the winter blues away with a *Simply Sensual*
tale…wonderful, alluring and fascinating!"
—*Romantic Times*

Available in January 2004.

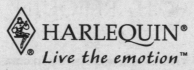

Visit us at www.eHarlequin.com

PHSSCP3

The Queen of Sizzle brings you sheer steamy reading at its best!

USA TODAY
Bestselling Author

LORI FOSTER

FALLEN ANGELS

Two full-length novels *plus* a brand-new novella!

The three women in these
stories are no angels…
and neither are
the men they love!

Available February 2004.

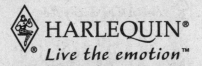

HARLEQUIN®
Live the emotion™

Visit us at www.eHarlequin.com

PHFA

is turning 20!

We're young, we're legal (well, almost) and we're old enough to get into trouble!

And to celebrate our coming of age, we're reintroducing one of our most popular miniseries.

Whenever you want a sassy, sexy book with a little something out of the ordinary, look for...

Editor's Choice

Don't miss February's pick...

COVER ME
by Stephanie Bond

It all started the day my best friends told me to get a life. Up to this point, my world centered around *Personality,* the magazine I work for. So, I had a one-night stand—an absolutely incredible one-night stand. It's a shame these things are supposed to be temporary. I thought it was all over...until I discovered the man I'd left in bed that morning was *Personality*'s latest cover model. And that I'd been assigned to keep an eye on him—day and night...

Available wherever Harlequin books are sold.

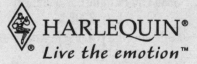

HARLEQUIN®
Live the emotion™

Visit us at www.eHarlequin.com

HTEC

HARLEQUIN®
Temptation

THE WRONG BED

What happens when a girl finds herself in the
wrong bed...with the *right* guy?

Find out in:

#866 NAUGHTY BY NATURE by Jule McBride
February 2002

#870 SOMETHING WILD by Toni Blake
March 2002

#874 CARRIED AWAY by Donna Kauffman
April 2002

#878 HER PERFECT STRANGER by Jill Shalvis
May 2002

#882 BARELY MISTAKEN by Jennifer LaBrecque
June 2002

#886 TWO TO TANGLE by Leslie Kelly
July 2002

Midnight mix-ups have never been so much fun!

HARLEQUIN®
Makes any time special ®

Visit us at www.eHarlequin.com

HTNBN2